Also by Sarah Wisseman:

The House of the Sphinx
The Fall of Augustus
Bound for Eternity
The Dead Sea Codex

3-12

The Bootlegger's Nephew

Sarah Wisseman

HILLIARD HARRIS

312
17⁰⁰

HILLIARD HARRIS

P.O. Box 275
Boonsboro, Maryland 21713-0275

ISBN 1-59133-372-5
978-1-59133-372-2

Book Design: S. A. Reilly
Cover Illustration © S. A. Reilly
Manufactured/Printed in the United States of America
2012

To my beloved stepmother, Janet Means-Underhill, and my beloved godparents, Joy and Dick Unsworth.

Acknowledgements:

This is my first historical mystery, so the writing journey has been one of discovery on several levels. Many people contributed to this book, either directly or indirectly. For wonderful stories about Illinois archaeology before it became a true academic discipline, I am grateful to Tom Emerson, Dale McElrath, Andy Fortier, Ken Farnsworth, and Doug Jackson, my colleagues and friends at the Illinois State Archaeological Survey at the University of Illinois in Urbana-Champaign. They gave me far more information than I could use in one book. It is not their fault that I used so little of this rich material or that I twisted the facts to suit my own ends, especially when Prohibition took over as the focus of the novel.

For help with local archives and artifacts, I thank the wonderful folks at the Urbana Archives and the Champaign County Historical Museum who answered my many questions. My grateful thanks to fellow Mystery Cat Molly MacRae, author of Lawn Order and Wilder Rumors, for her many careful readings and comments along the way, and Charlie Boast and Marsha Clinard for proofreading.

I could never have completed the manuscript without the encouragement, jokes, and medical information provided by my husband, Charlie Wisseman, who also read and commented on different stages of the manuscript. Thanks too to the other writers have contributed useful historical tidbits and helpful hints on technique: Jeanne Dams, Barbara D'Amato, Mary Whelk, and Tasha Alexander.

The Bootlegger's Nephew is set during the fall and winter of 1923, a mere three years after women achieved the vote (1920), just after the discovery of insulin (1922), only a few years after the great flu epidemic (1918-1919), and a year after the discovery of the Pharaoh Tutankamun's tomb in Egypt (1922). A few more items to set the stage for 1923: Calvin Coolidge was president, Time Magazine was founded that year, and the Ku Klux Klan held a huge rally in East St. Louis at Cahokia, Illinois. Prohibition was in full force throughout the U.S. A quart of beer cost about 80 cents, while a quart of gin was $6. A single drink could range in price from under a dollar (beer for 25 cents a bottle) to $1.50 or more, depending on the source of the booze.

For readers who are interested in more research on Prohibition in east-central Illinois, I plan to upload a non-fiction appendix to my website: www.sarahwisseman.com.

A SAMPLE OF TWENTIES SLANG

Applesauce!—Baloney!
Attagirl!—Well done!
Bags—as in "Oxford Bags": pants
Bee's Knees—excellent, first-rate (similar—cat's meow)
Blind Pig—hidden bar, often behind a false storefront (laundry, barbershop—tobacco shop, ice cream parlor, etc.)
Bootlegger—'legger: someone who transports liquor illegally
Bubs—breasts
Bushwa—bullshit
Butt me—I'll take a cigarette
Dead soldier—empty bottle
Giggle water—booze
Gin mill—speakeasy, especially a cheap one
Goat whiskey—Indian moonshine
Hayburner—gas-guzzling car
Hooch—booze, liquor
Jack—money
Jeepers Creepers!—Jesus Christ!
Juice joint—speakeasy
Let's ankle—let's get out of here
Moonshiner—amateur booze producer. Often an individual or family operation near a stream (water was needed to cool the mash)
Ossified—drunk
Rum-runner—someone who transports liquor illegally, especially over state borders or by boat.
Sap—fool
Sheba—girlfriend (from the popular movie "The Sheik")
Sheik—boyfriend (from the popular movie "The Sheik")
Spifflicated—drunk
Squiffy—drunk
Tomato—sexually ripe female
Tin Lizzie—Model T Ford automobile

Chapter One
Early on a Saturday morning in November

The patient's breath stank of fermented foods overlaid with cheap alcohol, burnt sugar, and iodine. The smell of bad booze—hardly Chicago's best yack-yack bourbon. Doc Junker figured it was probably the same coffin varnish available in every blind pig between Big Grove and Kankakee.

Good ole' Nathan Donaldson, car salesman, landowner, and looter of Indian graves, lay on the examining table in the former porch that served as Junker's home office. Cantankerous when sober, impossible when drunk, Nathan looked even worse than usual with sweat beading on his bony forehead. Donaldson's hired hands, Hank and Larry, had dragged him in from the icy November rain and roused the doctor and his wife from a cozy, down-covered bed.

Doc Junker sighed as he washed his hands in hot, soapy water. "Nate, what in tarnation have you been up to this time? Any reason why you can't get yourself shot at during office hours so I don't have to get up in the middle of the night?"

"Aw, Illinois, I didn't plan it that way!" Nathan gasped, shifting his gaze sideways. "We had a burglar out at Dad's farm and he was armed." He tried to shift his injured leg. "Oh...cat turds, it hurts!"

"Bushwa," said Junker. He didn't believe a word of it. Nathan's trousers were covered with dark splotches, as if he'd been kneeling in dirt. And he had filthy fingernails. Ten to one he'd been digging on someone else's property and the owner had shot him. Nathan and his son Frank shared Illinois

Junker's passion for archaeology, but only for what they could sell from the sites they looted and mangled. If Junker got there first, he made sketches of the layout and excavated small sections, bit by bit, recording everything and trying to picture the history of the people who'd lived and eaten and died on that spot. In contrast, the Donaldsons blasted through the layers looking for skulls and arrowheads and copper, scattering hearths and potsherds willy-nilly, making such a mess that no one who came after them could make any sense of it. Doc Junker was trying to convert Nathan to his systematic way of doing things, but it was an uphill battle; Nathan'd rather strip a site and pinch all the good stuff for himself instead of working with anyone else.

"So, you got shot on your own property, not nearby at Tate Farm, which we all know is a magnet for every criminal for miles around and all sorts of nefarious nocturnal activities?" Both properties lay just outside of Big Grove to the southeast, along the Salt Fork River. That put them not too far from the old saline springs that first drew entrepreneurs to Champaign County to mine salt.

"Aw, never mind where it happened—just take the bullet out, would ya? And dope me up good before you touch that leg. It's killing me," Nathan whined.

"Well, from the smell of you, Nate, you won't need ether or anything else. You're already spifflicated." Grabbing his scissors, Doc Junker carefully slit his patient's trousers from ankle to crotch. Nathan's thigh was discolored and blood encrusted near the bullet hole, but there was very little swelling. This was bread-and-butter medicine, something Junker could handle. At least it wasn't the screamin' meemies or the sort of abdominal wound he'd seen during the Great War in the trenches of France.

Junker sniffed the air as the welcome scent of fresh coffee infiltrated the room. Ah! An ambrosial whiff to offset the odors of sweat, dirty flesh, and bad hooch. His wife Martha was in the kitchen preparing hot drinks.

He leaned over the leg, prodding gently around the bullet hole.

"Hell and damnation!" cried his patient, kicking at Junker with his good leg.

Probably a cracked femur, with the bullet lodged on the left side of the thigh. "Cripes, Nathan! Do you want me to fix your leg or not?"

Nathan calmed down a mite, just as Martha Junker entered the room with a tray of coffee and *Springerle*. Her long blond braid lay like a fat snake over the shoulder of her wool robe. "Here, have something hot to drink," she said, offering steaming mugs to Junker and the two hired hands. "And today I baked these."

Admirable woman—Martha's baking and her nursing skills were well known all over Big Grove. Too bad her mind sometimes resembled an uncharted labyrinth to her husband of twenty years.

In short order, the hired hands descended on her offerings like starving guttersnipes.

"Hey, how about me?" said Nathan.

"Later," Junker said. "You can have cookies after I remove the bullet." He sure hoped Martha'd put aside some cookies for him.

"Can't you at least give me some hair of the dog?" Nathan muttered.

"You've had more than is good for you," Junker retorted. "How are you paying this time?"

"He ain't got no cash..." said Larry, the chunkier of the two hired hands.

"Says you," Junker replied. Nathan was known to be well off. He generated excellent sales with the newest Fords and Pathfinders as well as older models, and his family owned huge tracts of farmland outside Big Grove. But the man sure was cheap with his dollar bills.

"Honest, he told us he ain't got no cash on him. He's gonna pay you in artifacts." Larry pulled out a burlap bag and tipped some choice potsherds and a dark gray stone pipe with a carved otter onto the doctor's desk.

Junker grabbed the pipe and examined it, enjoying the smooth feel of the polished surface. Sure looked like Ohio stone, but he hadn't seen an otter before...

"Earl!" cried Martha, her blue eyes snapping and her hands perched on her ample hips. "Make Nathan pay cash! I can't keep the books for you if you let patients pay in dirty artifacts and hooch!"

Junker had certainly heard this complaint before. But if he did everything the way Martha wanted, he would have nothing left of his self-respect. Sometimes, like now, he just nodded in her general direction and went right on with what he was doing.

Martha was the only person who called him Earl, let alone his full name: Earl Snyder Junker. Usually it was "Doc Junker" or "Illinois," the nickname given to him by his fellow medics during his six-month stint in the Great War. The name had stuck when he returned home because of his abiding interest in Illinois history and archaeology.

Doc Junker fingered some pieces of carved and burnished pottery. "Where did you find these, exactly?" The Donaldson and Tate properties covered at least four square miles.

"Wouldn't you like to know, Illinois," wheezed his rival, "East of town, but I ain't tellin' you exactly where."

"Of course not." Junker looked closer at the pile of artifacts. "Hey, wait a minute! That's not ceramic!" He picked up a thin, curved piece with brown and black mottling and tilted it under the light. "It's a skull bone—human parietal by the look of it—and it's got carving on it. Dang it, Nathan! You've been digging another burial site!"

"So what? Aw, crap...quit talkin' and grousin' and patch me up."

"On your head be it, Nathan. I'll take out the bullet, but if it nicked the femur as I think it did, you're going to have a bum leg for quite awhile. I'm going to order you a Thomas splint, so you can get around your farm. Might be hard to come into town, though..."

"Just do it, and get it over with!"

Doc Junker pulled a sterile probe and his longest tweezers out of his ready tray. He eyed his patient—Nathan was still so intoxicated Junker couldn't give him either a sedative or ether.

4

That meant his ministrations were going to hurt like hell.

Junker nodded at Martha, who donned a clean white smock and took her place at the table as she had so many times before. "Hold him down," Junker said. "The bullet is going to take a bit of digging and it will hurt like blazes."

Hank, the skinny fella, moved to help Martha, taking the feet while she took the shoulders.

"ARGGGH!" cried Nathan, struggling in vain against the four hands and strong arms that held him down. Then he passed out.

The removal of the bullet took only five minutes. Doc Junker stitched up the wound with silk thread and placed a dressing over it.

Whew. He really hated operating on folks he knew, especially when he caused them pain. But Big Grove wasn't that large a town and that meant he often did work on friends, relatives, and neighbors—often because no other doctor was available. As he washed his hands in the tiny bathroom next to his surgery, he spoke to Nathan's men. "You'd better leave him here. I have an extra cot for patients who can't walk out of here right away. Leave me the otter pipe and the skull fragment as payment and come get him in the morning."

"Right, Doc." They helped him move Nathan to the cot by his desk and left, slamming the front door so hard that the glass panes rattled.

Martha, shaking her head in exasperation, picked up the coffee tray and headed for the kitchen at the back of the house. "Jumping Jehoshaphat!" she said, using Junker's father's favorite expression. "What a way to run a business! And the clientele gets worse all the time!"

Thomas Earl Junker, whose active family practice had included all classes of patients, would have agreed with her—and added some memorable descriptions of his own varied experiences. Those stories, enhanced by colorful expressions from the previous century, had infected the entire family, from Illinois and Martha down to the youngest twin.

Illinois Junker was just thinking fondly of the feather comforter and catching some sleep when he heard a key scratch in the door.

His daughter Anna staggered into the house, her arm curled around the waist of a dark-haired, slightly built man about her own height.

Junker's assistant and former comrade-in-arms, Tommy Crouch, was loaded to the muzzle and proud of it. Tommy was supposed to see that Anna got home safely, but it sure looked the other way round this time. Doc Junker would deal with him later, after he'd sobered up.

"Doc, you shoulda seen the fight! I belted him in the kisser, a good one! He practically spun a three-sixty and then..."

"Father, I'm sorry, but I didn't know what else to do with him," said Anna, panting with exertion. She shed her fur coat as Junker caught Tommy and shoved him into a handy chair.

"...he landed against the bar and I belted him again." Tommy smiled, a singularly sweet smile considering how zozzled he was.

Martha arrived with a rush, all her maternal instincts bristling and raring for a fight. "Anna! You've been at the speakeasies *again*, and now look at you! What happened this time?"

Anna did look like a rag-a-muffin. Her low-cut, knee-length dress was limp and creased where Tommy had leaned against her, and her blond curls looked tousled where they peeked out from the low brim of her felt cloche hat. Her beautiful face was rosy with whatever she'd had to drink. Probably Sugar Moon; that was her current favorite.

Junker groaned inwardly. His dear wife was about to make Anna's life a misery, and he knew better than to side openly with his daughter against Martha On-the-Warpath.

"Answer me, Anna Maria!" Martha said.

Anna sighed and took off her hat, perching it on a hook by the door. "We went to the Steamroom first but ended up at the Pickled Onion. You know the place, Father. It's usually smoky and noisy but not dangerous, and..."

"I suppose Sally talked you into going."

Sally McKinley was dark and voluptuous, a real tomato. A bit wild, but most girls were nowadays. Sally wasn't good for

6

Anna, but Junker figured Anna would decide that on her own—eventually. He had a high opinion of her intelligence and good sense—he just hoped she'd survive the normal teenage experience of trying on new roles and friends like costumes without getting into too much trouble. Anna was like him: she worked hard and she played hard. When not at her classes at the Julia F. Burnham School of Nursing or babysitting, Anna haunted the local speakeasies and dance halls.

"Mother, I was going anyway. What happened was, Sally finally told Frank Donaldson to beat it, but he got obnoxious and pushed Sally up against the bar..."

"*Lieber Gott!* That Sally is not a fit companion for you—always into trouble getting!" cried Martha. Her native German syntax crept back into her speech whenever she got upset.

"Oh, piffle, Mother! She's my best friend, and it's not her fault guys like her. She collects beaus like hats—one for every weekday, two on Sundays."

Junker intervened. "What happened with Frank, and how did Tommy get into it?" He kept his voice even so Anna wouldn't clam up on them; she was pretty sensible for nineteen, but Martha was not yet ready to admit it.

"Well, Tommy was pretty squiffy by then, but he saw that Sally was uncomfortable..." Her glance at her father said, *I'm giving you the expurgated version, Papa.* "Uh...so Tommy went up and punched him and they got into a swell...I mean, a big...fight. After Frank passed out and Tommy picked himself off the floor, I decided it was time to leave and we walked home."

Staggered home was more like it. Doc Junker looked at Martha. From her expression, she had plenty more to say. He cut her off at the pass. "Look, Anna, you're old enough now to go out with your friends, we both know that. But maybe you could make some of your excursions in daylight for a week or so. Go get ice cream at Vriner's or Vaky's, something harmless like that. Or at least steer Sally to a different speakeasy."

His wife and daughter spoke at the same time.

"Not another speakeasy! What are you saying, Earl? You know how I feel about my father's drinking..."

"All right, Papa. Do you think Sally could come over tomorrow and...?"

"Calm down, girls. We'll sort all this out in the morning. In the meantime, it's high time for bed."

Two more interruptions prevented Junker from getting his much longed for rest.

His daughter Emma, one of his two seven-year-old twins, burst into the room in her nightie. "Mama! Franz just threw up all over the rug in the hall!"

"I will come." Martha shook her head and hurried out, herding Emma before her.

Then someone else arrived on the doorstep and the front door quivered as if a battering ram were hitting it.

Junker flung open the door. His neighbor Linda Keck, a blanket wrapped around her tall form, stood on his top step.

"Doc? I just had a phone call from Sam Cunningham. He couldn't get through to your house; your phone must be off the hook. Sam's sister is in labor, and Jo Cunningham says it's not goin' well. She says, hurry."

Chapter Two
Same morning

Shrugging into his wool overcoat, Doc Junker grabbed his black bag and peaked cap. He exited the house and crossed the tiny lawn in darkness that was hushed and damp with the approaching dawn. He tripped slightly on an uneven brick at the edge of Elm Boulevard as the tall trees overhead funneled cold droplets of water down the back of his neck.

Soon he was driving east in his poorly heated Tin Lizzie—his Model T—eager to reach his friend's home. Gerry Cunningham owned and ran one of their most popular and well-equipped stores, "Cunningham's Drugs and Books," near the University of Illinois campus. He and his wife, Jo, lived southeast of Big Grove in a rambling white farmhouse that Martha and Junker had visited many times for dinner followed by piano-playing and singing in their charming parlor.

It was easy to see why early settlers shunned the lowlands around here in favor of slightly higher land with groves of trees. Every rainstorm left standing water in the fields, a reminder of the time when the whole county was a malaria-filled swamp. It took immigrants from northern Europe—Norwegians and Swedes and Dutch—to see the potential of such waterlogged land for farming.

"Mashaw Montuck, " or "Big Woods," was the Indian name for their first settlement up near Adkins Point to the north. Lewis Adkins built his home there in 1836. That was before the railroad that changed everything came to town. When the new depot was established on the west side of town to accommodate the train to and from Chicago, the population quadrupled in a decade. Now they had a decent-sized town, with hotels and restaurants and moving picture theaters.

Junker rolled his shoulders behind the wheel to loosen his back up. He should have been sleepy, but the impromptu surgery had jazzed him up—at least for a couple of hours. Besides, Doc Junker enjoyed driving through his hometown—especially in the pre-dawn while folks slept and the streets were quiet.

By the time he turned south on Route 130, the rain ceased and the sky paled in the east. A capricious wind skipped over the wet ground, scooping up stray leaves and flinging them into the air.

The landscape around Big Grove, east central Illinois, was as flat as a flapper's chest. 'Course young women's bosoms weren't really that flat, but the silly fools bound their breasts to achieve a more boyish look. Ridiculous, but as Anna said, "it's fashionable, Papa, so that's why we do it."

Central Illinois wasn't many people's idea of heaven, but Junker couldn't imagine living anywhere else. Outside of town, the fields of corn and prairie stretched all the way to the horizon and the tall grasses ruffled in the wind like an ocean. But the sky was vast. If he painted what he saw, the frame would be three-quarters sky and only one-third land. A big sky meant gorgeous sunsets—and if he were awake for them, even prettier sunrises.

Junker parked his vehicle in the Cunningham's driveway. He figured at least two of the children would be there, along with their parents. Sam worked at Cunningham's store, and his sister Elizabeth was living at home because her lover had deserted her the moment he found out she was pregnant.

A disheveled and worried Gerald Cunningham met Junker at the door with Sam looming just behind him. "Illinois, we need you! The baby's born, but we can't stop the bleeding!"

Dread settled in his gut. Uncontrollable hemorrhaging in a new mother was the worst of news. Junker hustled in as quickly as the narrow door and his gimpy leg—a relic of the Great War—allowed.

"Doc Junker! Thank God you've come." Josephine Cunningham's brown eyes showed strain and her lovely hair straggled from its usually neat bun. Jo was forty-two—two years older than Junker was. Her age seemed to have nothing to do with how attractive Junker found her. He spent most of his time in her presence savoring the way his blood raced and feeling guilty that he lusted after his best friend's wife.

Not now, though. Junker focused on the job to come and shoved every other feeling into what he called his emotional strongbox. That was the only way to deal with doctoring friends and relations.

She led him to the birthing room, still full of the stink of blood, sweat, and fetal fluids. Dark-haired Elizabeth Cunningham lay in a tangle of sheets, eyes closed, and her immobile face turned towards her brand-new daughter.

Jo lifted the baby, already clean and swaddled, and moved her to a nearby cradle while Junker examined the new mother. Elizabeth's face was drained of color and she barely responded to his touch. Gently, he removed the soiled sheet over her legs and saw blood seeping around a ragged tear in the perineum. He could repair the tear easily, but first he had to stop the bleeding.

"Jo, has the afterbirth come out?" He and Jo had worked together a year ago, when her other daughter, Alice, had borne a strapping baby boy. The chill on the back of his neck told him this was not going to be an equally happy occasion.

"Yes, a while ago. It's in that," she pointed at a blue enamel bowl.

Doc Junker examined the placenta, noting its small size and torn edge. Some of it must still be inside the uterus. He massaged Elizabeth's abdomen, hoping that the muscle would contract and the bleeding stop.

A vain effort. The seepage was relentless, and his patient now unconscious, her pallor tinged with blue. He had to get her to Burnham Hospital in time to try a transfusion, a fairly new procedure. Their two-way stopcock apparatus was only five years old, but his colleague Jim Harris was experienced with it. "Jo, call an ambulance. She needs a blood transfusion, and we'll need to move quickly. Do you know your family's blood types?"

Jo paled. "I'm type A positive, and Gerald is O, but I don't think we know Elizabeth's." She ran into the hallway and picked up the receiver.

"Wait," Junker said, listening to Elizabeth's shallow, irregular breathing. "I think we'd better try taking her in my Model T. It will be faster."

But not fast enough. By the time Gerry and Sam had settled Elizabeth in a cocoon of blankets in the motor vehicle, she was motionless.

"She's not breathing anymore!" cried Sam.

Hoping for a miracle, Junker took her pulse and listened to her chest. Nothing. He did it again, with the same result. Finally he straightened up and confronted the appalled faces of the Cunningham family.

"She's gone. I couldn't save her. I am so terribly sorry…"

Gerry and Junker carried Elizabeth back into the house and laid her gently on the sofa in the front parlor. Sobbing filled the room as Jo slumped in the nearest chair, holding the hand of her dead daughter while Sam crouched near his sister's body. Even in her grief, Jo was beautiful, like a slender tulip bending to the wind.

Next to Junker, Gerry stood like a statue, his face completely blank and his hands limp at his side. Junker put a hand on his shoulder and bowed his head, wishing he could dredge up some words of comfort. A black cloud of failure settled over his brain.

"Gerry…Jo…I wish I could have done something." *Anything, anything to save my best friend's daughter.*

Gerry sighed. "Not your fault, Illinois."

Doc Junker stayed a little longer, doing his meager best to comfort his friends.

As he drove back into town, fatigue and recriminations dogged him. If only they'd called him sooner! If only he'd gotten Elizabeth to the hospital! But the science of transfusion was still in its infancy; there was no guarantee that even if they'd made the thirty-minute journey that the procedure would have been a success. Rather he had to admit that birthing babies was still a risky business, despite all the medical advances since his father's time. They'd both lost so many young mothers...

At home, he found his wife kneading bread dough and listening to the radio. Adolf Hitler's recent attempt at a *coup d'etat* at a bar in her native Munich was the subject of the broadcast, causing Martha to thump the dough with unusual force on the counter. She took one look at his face and said, "What happened?"

He told her.

"Oh, Earl, not Elizabeth! How awful." Tears filled her blue eyes.

"I did everything I could, but it wasn't enough."

She patted his arm. "Go to bed. The hospital doesn't need you until two, and there's no one waiting in the surgery. I'll call you."

He was too exhausted to argue. He trudged upstairs, shucked off shoes and trousers, and buried himself under the pile of covers.

Chapter Three
Saturday evening

Cigarettes. Booze. Sweat.

Anna's nose tingled from the familiar smells. The speakeasy's name, "The Steamroom," fit only too well. It lurked behind a commercial laundry and next to a smithy on Hickory Street. The overheated, smoky room made folks' skin gleam with perspiration, and the fourteen kinds of beer, gin, and whiskey generated heat—and hot air—in their insides.

Although Vriner's Confectionery, just two blocks away, boasted a fancy marble bar and leather-topped stools, this juice joint was definitely a cut below. Here, the linoleum counter fought with rough round tables and chairs made of pine—cheap materials for a semi-public watering hole. Anyone over the age of sixteen who could pay for a drink and knew the "speak-easy" password was welcome to come on in.

Anna, wearing a sleek purple dress with a fringed hem and fake pearls, shoved her way past laughing young men and giggling girls in search of Sally McKinley, who'd disappeared fifteen minutes earlier claiming she was going to "visit the powder room."

"Anna! Let me buy you a drink."

Uh oh. She tilted her chin at a tall man with sleek black hair and an engaging grin. This fella was more Sally's friend than Anna's—like most of the men hovering around the bar.

"In a minute, Steve. I'm going to the powder room. And I don't want any of that tarantula juice you got me last time!"

"Don't worry, I'll get you something that won't rot your

delicate insides."

Someone changed the radio station, and several voices joined in singing, "*Yes! We Have No Bananas!*"

Anna met Sally coming from the back corridor, her lipstick smeared. "Oh ho! Who's the lucky guy?"

"Mind your potatoes," said Sally, avoiding her eyes.

A lipstick-stained Benjamin Keck appeared behind her, looking sheepish.

Anna felt as if she'd been kicked in the stomach. Sally had been kissing Ben! Ben Keck, the boy next door, was the only man Anna really liked. But he had no eyes for her, only Sally. Sally could have anyone—why, oh why did she have to pick on Ben?

To be fair, Anna hadn't actually told Sally she was interested in Ben, so in the language of best girlfriends, he was fair game. Maybe she should tell Sally to screw off, but the thought of the inevitable teasing and sly looks in front of the others made Anna cringe. Sally had trouble keeping secrets; she enjoyed the limelight too much. And Anna's feeling for Ben was too new, too special, to expose to the rest of the world just yet.

Anna eyed Sally with reluctant envy, watching her reapply her scarlet lipstick to her fashionably bow-shaped lips. Sally's straight, shiny black hair cut in a Dutch bob and olive skin made her look exotic, and her hourglass figure assured her plenty of attention. Anna's slender figure appeared boyish by comparison, and she thought her blond curls were too "ordinary."

Sally capped her lipstick and slid it into her beaded bag. "I need a drink," she said, gliding up to the bar in her low-backed ivory sheath and heeled Mary Janes.

Wouldn't a true best friend be less callous? Wouldn't a true best friend refrain from annexing every eligible man in the vicinity, including the fella I want?

Anna was a bit surprised at the disloyal voice in her head. She often felt as if she had another, stronger person inside her, struggling to burst forth and tell the world what was what. That other person was more sophisticated, not so shy and comfortable in her own skin.

15

Steve Busey was ready with two tall glasses, handing one to each of them. Sally took a deep swig of her drink.

Anna hesitated. "What's this?" she asked, examining the deep red color of the liquid.

"Gin and fruit juice—grape and cranberry or some such," said Steve with a wink. "Try it, toots."

"Oh. Thanks." Anna sipped her drink, suddenly feeling out of place, as if she'd walked into a dance hall wearing the wrong kind of dress or clunky shoes. Maybe it was the incident with Ben and Sally, or maybe she felt a tad guilty that she and Sally had ignored her father's advice about avoiding the speakeasies for a while. And Steve always made her self-conscious. At twenty-one, he was only two years older than Anna, but he looked so polished, with his V-necked sweater vest over white flannels and slicked down hair parted in the middle. His smooth baritone oozed confidence, and he attracted girls without even trying.

Now he slanted his dark eyes down at her and grinned. "Well, what do you think?"

Anna took another cautious sip. "It's kinda sour, don't you think?"

Steve laughed, and his buddy with the fedora suggested the barkeeper give her some sugar "to sweeten her up."

Anna covered her discomfort with a smile and turned towards the door, leaning her elbows against the bar in what she hoped was a casual but sexy pose.

Frank Donaldson tripped as he entered the bar area and made a beeline for Sally.

Oh, no! Anna cringed. Last night, she'd stupidly gotten involved. She'd stepped between Frank and Sally when Frank got rowdy. Instead of grabbing Sally, Frank'd shoved Anna up against the bar, clutching her behind as he belched gin fumes into her face. That's when Tommy Crouch had barged in and shoved Frank into the center of the main room of Pickled Onion so he could belt him one.

This time, Ben Keck saved Sally and Anna from embarrassment. Spotting Frank weaving his way towards trouble, he strode over and grabbed his buddy by the elbow.

16

"Frank! C'mon over to our table! I've already got some of your favorite tipple ready for you."

"Gotta speak to my girl. Sally! Gotta tell her about my plans 'cause soon I'll be rich! C'mere, honey!" Frank eyes bulged as Steve grabbed his other elbow. Together, Ben and Steve steered him to a small table in the corner.

Frank Donaldson getting rich? Anna didn't believe it for a moment—the guy spent everything he earned. Frank was such a goof; if he was coming into real money, chances were it was for doing something on the wrong side of the law. Ben acted like he was a friend of Frank's, but what did that say about Ben's ability to judge people?

Sally, oblivious to her near miss, went right on flirting with an older fella Anna had never seen before. She didn't even turn around.

The inner door from the smithy swung open again and a familiar voice said, "Make us some space! My companion is ill." A middle-aged man with a full beard and a bit of a paunch supported a stocky fella who could barely walk.

It was Illinois Junker with his friend Harold Stipes, a reporter for the local newspaper.

"Father!" Anna cried, running over to the two men. What a relief to have something to do besides lounging around pretending she was having a good time. "How can I help?"

"Push this table out of the way," her father said. "I think Harry's having a heart attack, but I want to lay him down on the floor before he hurts himself." Doc Junkers yelled at the bartender, "Call for an ambulance!"

Anna shoved the table and chairs back, making a rough circle on the filthy wooden floor. To her surprise, Ben Keck helped her. As she knelt next to Mr. Stipes to take his pulse, she felt a professional interest in assessing the sick man's symptoms—heavy breathing and blue lips, on the verge of unconsciousness. And a little vomit on his coat lapel.

Doc Junker, still wearing his hat, loosened Stipes' stiff collar and unbuttoned the top of his shirt. "Hang on, Harry," he muttered, using his elbows to hold back the legs of interested bar patrons. "Give the poor man room to breathe!" he shouted.

Ben Keck stood up and held his arms wide to encourage patrons to move back.

Harold Stipes responded by opening his eyes, which bulged, and gasping for air. "Ah...ah...ah...eh...eh...eh!" Suddenly he surged up against Doc Junker's restraining arm, gurgled loudly, and fell back on the floor with a thud.

His breath stopped but his eyes remained open.

Anna's father immediately tried to resuscitate him by pumping with both hands on his chest, but Stipes remained unresponsive.

"Damn," whispered Junker, sitting back on his heels and hanging his head. He pulled out a large, cotton handkerchief and wiped his sweaty forehead.

Anna noticed his usually steady hands were shaking. No wonder—he'd failed to save his friend. And she knew he'd already lost another patient, a young mother, this week...

She caught Ben's horrified gaze.

The crowd surged forward again.

"Is he still alive?"

"Who is it? I can't see."

"What's going on?" asked Joe the bartender, elbowing his way through.

Doc Junker stood up and had a whispered conference with him. "I recommend moving him—is there another room where we can wait for the medics?"

"Yeah." Joe motioned to a server and Ben to help him and the three men carried Stipes through the side door into the steam laundry. Joe glanced at Anna. "I know this girl. Who is she, Doc?"

"My daughter—she's a nursing student. She's helping me," said Dr. Junker.

"Okay," Joe said with relief. "C'mon guys, back to work."

Anna shut the door after the three men, abruptly cutting off the sounds of revelry. The smoky fug of the speakeasy was replaced by heavy, moist air and swirling steam. Her father squatted on the floor, going through his friend's pockets. He put the wallet aside. Then he pulled out a dirty handkerchief, a pipe and tobacco pouch, a bulbous little flask, and a folded square of

18

newsprint and spread them in a neat row on the floor.

"Papa, what are you doing? Why empty his pockets?" Anna discovered that Ben was still there, kneeling right next to her.

"Shhh. It looks like Harry died of a heart attack, but he had some other symptoms outside...I wonder..."

"What do you mean?" A shiver ran down her bare arms.

The amber-colored flask boasted a blue label with flowing script: "Blue Fire...." The rest of the name was missing, but the label itself was adorned with a sketch of the common local prairie grass, Big Blue Stem. Doc Junker screwed off the cap and sniffed. His eyes met Anna's.

"Same crap my chum Nathan Donaldson was drinking the other night. Smells like iodine and burnt sugar, but I'm going to get it tested."

"Why? Isn't it just homemade hooch?"

"No. I think it's some kind of alcoholic home remedy, and I've seen several other patients with bottles like this in recent weeks."

"Sir, what do you think is in it?" Ben asked.

Doc Junker eyed him soberly. "Nothing good. Certainly alcohol, maybe cocaine, some herbs. But whatever this concoction is, it interacts with the medicine I prescribed and may have contributed to Stipes' death."

"So you'd like to know where this Blue Fire stuff came from, right?" said Ben.

"Yep, I sure would."

Anna reached over and unfolded the piece of newsprint. "It's a photograph—some fella in a fedora."

Her father took it from her and studied it. "Looks vaguely familiar. Hmm. I'm going to keep it. Both of you, keep your traps shut." He slid both flask and paper into his own capacious front pocket.

She and Ben nodded.

The door crashed open and two medics appeared with a stretcher, along with a burly man Anna recognized as "Big Bruce" Donaldson, Nathan's older brother and the owner of both the smithy and the speakeasy.

"Well, well, look what the cat dragged in. Illinois Junker!"

Bruce said, jovially. "What brings you here?" He loomed over Anna, his thinning hair catching the light like horse piss on a cobbled street.

"Harry Stipes and I were walking back to my car when he took ill—we came into your joint so I could treat him. But I was too late." Her father's shoulders slumped.

"What'd he die of?"

"Heart problems," Junker said shortly.

He'd once told Anna that "heart failure" was the ultimate cause of most deaths, so "heart problems" was a good, catchall diagnosis when you weren't sure what was really going on. Or when you didn't feel like discussing it in front of present company.

"Huh," said Donaldson, his squinty brown eyes scrutinizing Junker's face. "Well, corpses aren't good for business. Let's get him out of here—I gotta business to run." His gaze switched to Anna, moving insolently up and down her body.

"And who's this little smarty?"

Anna's cheeks flushed as her father took her arm and Ben hovered protectively on the other side.

"My daughter, Anna—one of your best customers, in case you hadn't noticed. And this young fella is our neighbor, Ben Keck. Come along, you two. I'll take you home before I stop by the hospital to file my report on poor Harry Stipes. Donaldson, the ambulance is here so we're ready to move the body..."

"Whaddya mean, move the body? Not before I've had a looksee." The speaker was a tall scarecrow of a man with thinning hair on top and a small, scraggly mustache that looked like an afterthought pasted onto his upper lip. He wore the uniform of a police captain.

Bruce Donaldson's face closed down. "Well, well, Captain Stoltman. Fancy meeting you here."

Johann Stoltman, a.k.a "Han the Hun," gave a nasty smile. "Trying to pull a fast one, Big Bruce? I just happened to be at the bar and I heard all the commotion. Who is this fella, and what happened?" He nodded at the body on the floor.

Doc Junker explained all over again. "Stipes was a heart patient of mine, so I will write the death certificate."

"Heart attack?" asked Stoltman.

"Sure looks like it," Junker agreed. "I was just about to have him moved to the hospital and start the paperwork."

"Make sure I get a copy," Stoltman said, hitching up his suspenders over his skinny belly. "And don't forget to notify the coroner."

"Don't try to teach me my business, Stoltman. Ben, Anna, let's get out of here." Doc Junker jammed his hat on his head and put an arm around Anna.

Anna wobbled a bit as she moved towards the exit. Her knees suddenly felt like her mother's *spaetzle* noodles—soft and pliable. She was stunned by the sudden death, but at the same time her heart thumped with excitement—Ben had helped! Father was going to drive them home, together!

Her elbow tingled where Ben gripped it to guide her to the Tin Lizzie. Vaguely, she wondered why Papa's tone with Big Bruce had been so gruff. Usually, her diplomatic father was polite to everyone.

But Papa suspected his friend Stipes had died from something besides a heart attack.

And he hadn't shown the photograph to police Captain Stoltman.

Ben Keck felt a surge of hope. Anna hadn't objected to his presence—she seemed to welcome him, as did her father. He'd been looking for an opportunity to get to know the enticing girl who'd lived next door most of his life, but his friend Frank Donaldson took a great deal of his free time, and Frank was part of Sally's wild crowd. Sally—an awfully slick girl, but what a vamp. That little incident in the hallway at the Steamroom— he hadn't kissed Sally, she'd kissed him and deliberately smeared her lipstick on his face. Then she made darn sure Anna saw them. Maybe because she suspected Ben wasn't part of her entourage of male admirers and she couldn't stand to have a fella show interest in any other girl. Anna deserved a better friend than that.

Now maybe he could put things with Anna on a different footing, establish a friendship that was more than just neighborly. He wanted her to see him as an interesting prospect, not just the boy-next-door who happened to work as a furniture salesman in his dad's business.

Ben was twenty-one. He'd just graduated from the University of Illinois the previous spring and started at Keck Furniture over the summer. He wasn't sure selling was quite his thing, but his dad was so keen to have him on board that he could hardly refuse. Besides, he hadn't figured out anything else to do with his life. When he wasn't at work, he took photographs of Big Grove, specializing in architectural features shot at odd angles and developed the black-and-whites in the darkroom he'd created in a corner of the Keck basement. He owned a Kodak No. 2 Brownie but was saving up for a German camera—hopefully a Leica. Maybe he could sell some photos to the local newspaper...and write a news feature to go with it. He'd always been an "A" student in English, and journalism intrigued him.

Now he waited for Doc Junker to unlock the Tin Lizzie, planning to bag a seat next to Anna. But her father opened the passenger door and settled Anna in the seat next to him. Anna turned her head and gave Ben an apologetic smile, which gave him hope.

On the way home, the three of them were almost silent. Ben figured Anna was still in shock and the doctor was beating himself up over not saving his friend. All too soon, they'd pulled into the Junker driveway.

"Would you like to come in, for a drink or something?" Anna asked shyly. "My mama baked today."

Hot Dawg! An invitation to the Junker inner sanctum!

"Sure," he said. He hoped his voice sounded suave and assured and that she couldn't hear his heart slamming around in his chest. "I've heard about Mrs. Junker's baked goods, especially her *springerle.*"

"Come on, then." Anna pulled her fur coat tightly around herself as they trooped up the back stairs into the kitchen. The rich smell of meat and onions from a recent meal met Ben's nose and his stomach growled.

Anna turned around and smiled at him. "Ooo! You must be

hungry! I'll fix you up. But we'll have to be quiet. My mama and the little ones are asleep."

While Anna hung their coats in the cloakroom and put a plate of cookies on the table, Ben took a seat at the kitchen table and studied his surroundings. A comfortable room, equipped with the latest gadgets like an electric toaster and a fancy stove, but with lacy white curtains and a German cuckoo clock to keep it from looking too much like the Sears Catalogue. The tablecloth was a practical, easy-to-wipe blue oilcloth, and the whole effect was cheerful and clean.

Then he looked at Anna.

She was making hot chocolate. He smiled, thinking how appealing she was, with her slim figure and blond curls. Her beautiful blue eyes and perfect skin mesmerized him. Unlike Sally the Vamp, everything about Anna was understated instead of flamboyant. Her curves were feminine but not lush, her clothing was tasteful rather than eye-popping, and her manner just a bit shy. What Ben liked best about her was the mobility of her features, the way expressions flitted across her face like shadows on the grass on a sunny day. Although the man in him imagined her naked, bathing with a bowl and a cloth as in an old painting, his photographer's mind saw her in a floor-length dress, posed gracefully with a hand on the mantelpiece.

She caught him looking at her and blushed. "It's hot chocolate—I hope that's ok. Seemed like the right thing after seeing someone...collapse like that."

Ben took the steaming mug and reached for a sugar cookie. "Thanks. It's perfect. Do you want to talk about what happened at the Steamroom? Or do you want to forget about it for awhile?"

She frowned. "I don't know. Father is disturbed about it, and I think maybe we should wait for him."

As if on cue, Doc Junker entered the kitchen and took a glass from the cupboard over the refrigerator. He poured a modest tot of Canadian bonded whiskey into it, and leaned against the counter. "I know you both are upset about Stipes' death. I am too—and I hope I find out that he died naturally and that he wasn't assisted into the next world by whatever was in that bottle."

"Doc, do you think that bottle contained one of those 'health tonics' peddlers sell door-to-door?" Ben asked.

"Very likely."

"How are those tonics made?" asked Anna.

Doc Junker smiled ruefully. "Well, you start with plain old water, cheap alcohol, and then add flavorings, like juniper berries, fruit extracts, bitters, and God knows what else. Probably drugs, too. "

"Huh," said Ben. "How much alcohol, sir?"

"Enough to make folks buy the products, that's for sure. According to the law, the amount of alcohol is supposed to be listed—but regulation is spotty at best."

"So," Ben continued. "The Volstead Act—Prohibition— means anything containing alcohol is big business..."

"Certainly. People, especially women who might not feel comfortable going to a speakeasy, can buy this stuff from peddlers and pretend they're imbibing something healthy while they get a little spifflicated. Darn fools." Doc Junker put his glass in the sink and turned around to face them. "This stuff keeps cropping up—makes my job harder. I'd like to get the contents of the flask tested before we speculate too much about what happened to Harry Stipes. He had some symptoms I don't understand..."

"Like what, Papa?" That was Anna.

Junker looked at her grimly. "Like seeing yellow. A kind of distorted vision, called *xanthopsia*." He frowned at both of them. "This is in confidence, understand, you two? Don't talk about it outside this room."

"I understand, Papa."

"Sure thing, Doc Junker."

"I'll say goodnight, then. I still have case notes to write before I can sleep. Anna, don't forget to turn off the lights."

"I won't.

Doc Junker left and immediately the room became cozier. Ben realized that with the topic of Stipes' death off limits, Anna would have to talk about herself.

It was all turning out swell.

Chapter Four
Monday

Doc Junker slept badly, tormented by memories of Harry's contorted face and the ache in his left leg caused by five-year old shrapnel—one of his unwelcome legacies from the Great War.

While Martha snored peacefully next to him, he flopped and fidgeted in the bed. The sour reek of failure was all too familiar to him—even the best doctors lost patients—but this time felt different. Harry had been a real friend, one of the few that Illinois had time for besides Gerry Cunningham. Harry was interested in everything around him, making him a great source of local lore and gossip. They'd often met for a quick drink at Hell's Half Acre or The Steamroom at the end of a hard day.

Junker had no idea what had actually killed Stipes, but he was determined to find out. Weakness, pain across the chest, nausea—these were all heart attack symptoms. But just before the two buddies had entered the speakeasy, Harry had complained of "seeing yellow." Those must have been his last words, because his face had purpled and the choking started. Poor Harry, what a way to go.

Junker hadn't told Anna and Ben, but yellow vision could be a sign of digitalis overdose. So had Harry overdosed himself with the medicine Junker had prescribed for him? Junker knew only too well how easy it was to forget if you'd taken your medicine or not when it was part of your daily routine. Digitalis was one of the most dangerous medicines he knew of—the correct dosage was beneficial, but even a little extra could cause problems.

Or had Harry's medicine interacted with that Blue Fire junk, whatever it was? Only way to be sure was to order an autopsy and to get the contents of the bottle tested.

And who was the fella in the newspaper photo? Junker knew he'd seen that face somewhere before, but his memory was acting sluggish and uncooperative.

He punched his feather pillow into a squashy square and prayed for sleep.

By six-thirty in the morning, Doc Junker was on the road to the Tate Farm, un-rested and unenlightened.

"What's eating you today, Doc?" asked Tommy Crouch. His voice sounded cheerful but his red eyes and pasty skin betrayed his tippling activities the previous evening.

"Lost another patient," Junker said grumpily. "And no, I don't want to talk about it."

"Sorry, Illinois," Tommy said in his nicest voice. "I know that upsets you—I sure don't like it when we lose people. Makes me feel useless and sad."

Junker sighed, throwing a sideways glance at Tommy's thin face with its straight-as-a-stick brown hair drooping over his forehead. "I know the feeling—a common one in this profession." He changed gears. "Dang, I'm not concentrating very well today. Did I miss the turn?"

"Left after that grove of maple and elm trees," said Tommy, who carried maps and landmarks in his head with ease. Having a hangover didn't seem to impair him much. "What's in store for us today?"

Doc Junker turned into the long dirt driveway leading to the Tate Farm.

"Checking on a broken foot I set a week ago—one of the farmhands."

"Couldn't he have come into the surgery?"

"No transport. Besides, I want check out the farm while we're out this way."

Tommy nodded. He was accustomed to his employer's insatiable curiosity about local landowners and property. He'd helped on numerous occasions with archaeological forays all over Champaign County. And he couldn't remember how many times Doc Junker had accepted pottery, carved pipes, shell beads and the like instead of cash for services. No wonder his boss had the best archaeological collection in Big Grove.

The two men passed several groups of dilapidated outbuildings that spanned at least two generations of Tates. Most were set well back from the road and gleamed white with hoarfrost in the early morning light. The Tate house, a substantial dwelling with two floors and a wrap-around porch, loomed on their right about forty yards from a run-down red barn. Junker parked in the clearing in front of the barn.

A dark head poked out of the side door. "Seth's in here," shouted one of the Tate boys—Dick, Junker thought, but he couldn't see the fella's face. Doc Junker grabbed his black bag, and followed by Tommy, entered the wooden building.

A blond-haired youth of about twenty was pitchforking hay into mangers, moving slowly because of the cast on his foot.

"Good morning, Seth. I hope you're not putting too much weight on that cast."

"No, Doc. I do some of my chores and then lay down awhile."

He put down his pitchfork and perched on a cask so Doc Junker could examine his leg. The swelling around the top of the cast had decreased—a good sign that healing was progressing—and the foot was protected by an overlarge rubber boot and two pairs of woolen socks.

Junker removed both socks and checked the color of Seth's foot and made him wiggle his toes. "You're in good shape. The cast can come off in five weeks or so—until then, don't get it wet, and keep your weight off it as much as possible."

"Yessir."

"Tommy, you write up the case notes and check in with Martha to see if there are any more calls." Their patients were accustomed to them using the telephone to call Junker's wife or Sarah, the operator, for messages. "I'll be outside."

"Sure thing, Illinois," Tommy pulled out his black notebook and uncapped his fountain pen.

Junker stepped out into the yard, enjoying the crisp air and weak sunshine on his face. This was one of his favorite parts of Champaign County; the undulating land reminded him of his cousin's farm in Indiana. He strolled away from the barn, setting his sights on a cluster of older buildings and a grove of maples near the Salt Fork River.

Now was his chance to figure out where Nathan Donaldson had found his artifacts. Junker had spotted him and his son Frank out this way once before, exploring along the riverbed. It was a part of the county Junker had intended to survey himself, since the Salt Fork fed into the Vermilion River over by Danville. Moundbuilder artifacts had been found by collectors further east and north of Big Grove, so why not here? Everything he'd read indicated ancient peoples lived close to the rivers that were rich sources of fish, mussels, and drinking water.

The closer Junker got to the riverbank, the muddier it became. Must be from all that rain they'd had two nights before. He tramped over uneven ground near what looked like a fifty-year-old farmhouse, now abandoned, and a barn of the same vintage. A shiny new padlock on the door showed that it was still in use.

While gazing at the upper branches of a magnificent oak next to an outbuilding, Junker stepped backward into a hole. Picking himself up, he spied several haphazard pits closer to the river. Aha—must be where the Donaldsons had been digging. He pulled out his collection bag, a small trowel, and a magnifying lens and dropped to his knees.

Soon he had uncovered several thick, gritty potsherds, a heap of mussel shells from an ancient midden, a pile of animal bones (beaver?) and a human femur. His excitement grew; the site might be some kind of prehistoric campsite with a burial nearby. After all, Nathan had found a skull fragment. Looking around him, Junker found it hard to understand why the Donaldsons had abandoned the job so quickly with so many artifacts left behind. Had they been interrupted?

"Hey, Illinois! There you are."

He turned at the sound of Tommy's voice. "Come and see

29

what I found," Doc Junker said. "Might be a major find here."

"First, get a look at this," said Tommy, holding out a squat little bottle the same shape and color as the one Junker had pulled out of Harold Stipes' pocket.

"Ha!" Junker said, taking it from him. The label was missing, but he opened the stopper and sniffed. "That burnt sugar smell—again," he muttered. "Where'd you find it, Tommy?"

"Inside the small white barn, near the door."

"Hang onto it for me, will you? Now it's my turn to amaze you." Junker showed Tommy the cache of artifacts.

Tommy whistled. "Your home museum is looking better already."

Junker smiled. Most of his collection consisted of ax heads and arrow points—very early tools and weapons from the time before settlements, when hunters roamed Illinois. But he was gradually building up some choice pieces of Moundbuilder stuff from his forays into the Illinois River valley and from trading with other archaeology enthusiasts throughout the state.

"Yup. Tommy, why don't you go back to the car and fetch some…"

Crack.

"What the hell?" said Tommy, whipping around.

"Duck!" Junker yelled at him, grabbing his sleeve and throwing himself flat in the loose dirt. "Some idiot is shooting at us."

After a couple of moments, Junker raised his head enough to yell, "Lay off, Donaldson! I won't hurt your precious site. Let's make a deal about the artifacts, okay?"

A second bullet slammed into the ground near by his left foot.

Jumping Jehoshaphat! Nathan and Frank liked to scare their archaeological rivals by shooting over their heads when they got too close to the goodies, but this was going a bit too far.

Tommy and Junker crawled into the shelter of another large oak tree, a monster that looked at least a hundred years old. Junker listened for further shots, but nothing happened.

Odd. He'd expected one of the Donaldsons to show himself

and apologize. "Nate! Frank! It's Illinois Junker and Tommy Crouch here. We're leaving the premises, so show some sense and quit shooting!"

Silence.

They waited ten minutes and then hot-footed it back to the Tin Lizzie.

Junker planned to give Nathan Donaldson an earful at the earliest opportunity.

Chapter Five
Tuesday

Thank goodness, it was her day off. No classes, no babysitting for the Harris family's trio of little terrors.

Anna was hungry. She padded down to the kitchen to grab some milk and leftover strudel. Her feet in their felt slippers skated across the black-and-white linoleum (the very latest thing in flooring, according to her mother) and opened the new refrigerator. As she filled her glass, she glanced around at the other features Martha was so proud of: the four-legged, white sink, with built-in draining board, and the fancy new stove (shiny black, with a white control panel on the front). "Progressive," the kitchen catalogue had said, but to Anna's eyes it was all a bit clinical. Reminded her of the hospital. The old kitchen had been so cozy with its sky blue and silver stove, colorful rag rugs and navy blue cupboards.

What should she do with her free time? Anna took her plate and wandered into the dining room. They'd moved the upright piano in there when Grandpa moved in two years earlier. She set plate and glass on the top of the Wurlitzer piano, next to Martha's Teco vases, and opened the latest issue of *Etude Music Magazine*. At twenty-five cents, it took a chunk out of her babysitting money, but it was chock full of sheet music, tips on music theory, and interesting articles. There was even a hilarious short story about a little girl who talked with musical instruments called "Betty and the Brass Instruments." She turned to an etude by Hartmann called "The Wandering Sprite," and played the first page.

After a few stumbles, she flipped the magazine shut and ate the last of her strudel, savoring the tartness of the apples. She couldn't concentrate on the music. Her mind kept replaying the scene in the speakeasy...Mr. Stipes' purple face and bulging eyes. The distress her father showed. The feeling of utter futility while watching someone die, and not being able to do a single thing to save him.

Time to talk with Grandpa. He always had a unique perspective, and Anna enjoyed taking advantage of the knowledge that she was his favorite grandchild.

She left her unwashed dishes on the new sink (she'd hear from Mama about that later) and entered the parlor, once a formal entertaining room but now refurbished as a bed-sitting room for her grandfather. The family still gathered around the radio cabinet to listen to programs and keep Grandpa company. They kept a fire going in there all year except in high summer.

As expected, her favorite relative was settled in cozy comfort near the east window with newspaper, his pipe and cherry tobacco, and a mug of his favorite English tea. Anna tiptoed around the wing chair so she could see past his luxuriant whiskers. Was he dozing? She could never be sure.

"Grandpa?"

The old man jumped slightly, and the Big Grove Gazette slid off his lap. "Yes, my sweet?"

Anna picked up the paper and put it on the table next to him. "How do you tell if someone's been poisoned? I mean, accidentally? By taking an overdose of something, or maybe combining a medicine with something else?"

Thomas Earl Junker stared at Anna from under his bushy white eyebrows. "An odd question from you, young lady. Have you seen something you shouldn't have?"

"Yeah...Saturday night. I was out with Father."

He peered at her face. "You look kind of pale, honey. Sit down, why don't you."

Anna pulled up the velvet hassock and sat where she could admire the way her grandfather's bushy eyebrows leapt around on his forehead. "I was at this speakeasy with Sally..."

Doc Junker, Sr. listened intently while Anna described the

untimely demise of Harold Stipes. "Blue lips, eh? Did he vomit or froth at the mouth?"

"There was a little vomit. And a little frothing, just before he expired. I don't know what happened before he came in with Papa."

"And what did your papa say?"

"He found a flask in Stipes' pocket. Seemed to think there was more than liquor in it, and that it might have aggravated Harry's bad heart."

"Well, overdosing and accidental poisoning have always been part of medical practice—goes with the territory. Mind you, I didn't see too many cases in my practice. There were so many other ways to die while I was growing up and learning to be a physician—childbirth, childbed fever, infection, gangrene...actually, infection sums up most of it. Did you know, young lady, that before the germ theory of medicine was well known—and that was well after the Civil War—doctors and medical students didn't even wash their hands between patients?"

"You can't go to nursing school and not hear about the importance of washing your hands, Grandpa," Anna said with a smile. "But I know using antiseptics and hand-washing wasn't common until the late 1800s." She also knew she was in for a spate of medical reminiscences, but she didn't mind. She always learned something new.

"Yep. I was knee-high to a mosquito when germs were accepted. Most surgeons thought it was all hot air. If they'd believed Oliver Wendell Holmes when he gave his paper on childbed fever in 'forty-three, my sister Suzanne might still be alive today."

"I read that surgeons were still operating in street clothes as late as the 1870s."

"That's right...I certainly saw that when I was training. Doctors in frock coats, covered with blood, moving from one bed to the next and in and out of surgery without changing." He grimaced. "My brother Gregor..."

"Your older brother. He was wounded in Maryland, right, Grandpa?"

"Yes, at Boonsboro in 'sixty-three, poor sap." Grandpa closed his eyes for a moment. "'Course there weren't any good drugs then, either. A stomach wound in wartime was an almost certain death sentence."

"You were too young for that war, right Grandpa?"

"I coulda gone—I was fourteen in 'sixty-two—but there was too much to do on the farm."

He sounded kind of regretful about that.

"Back to overdoses, Grandpa..." said Anna, rolling a little bit of yarn she'd found on the rug between her fingers.

"What's that about overdoses?" said her father, entering the room briskly. He dropped his black bag on the floor and built up the fire. Then he took a chair next to Anna.

"Papa! I told Grandpa about Mr. Stipes," said Anna. "And that you thought something in that flask might have hastened his demise."

Her father shot a sharp glance at her. "Hmm. Seems like I talked out of both sides of my mouth that night." He turned to Junker, Sr. "Dad, how are you today?"

"We...aall, my ticker is a bit jumpy, but you say that's normal. I feel okay considerin' I was seventy-five last week. I daresay I've got some time left—I'm not hanging up my fiddle just yet." He winked at Anna.

Illinois Junker smiled. "You are long-lived for your generation, Dad. Why look how many things you've survived—cholera, heart disease, influenza..."

"Dang it, don't even mention that epidemic to me," growled Grandpa. "I reckon I lost twenty or more friends in 1918, not to mention my last surviving relative." He shook his head dismally and began to fill his pipe.

Anna watched his gnarled, blue-veined hands perform the loving ritual of adding tobacco and tamping it down just so. With a pang, she noticed those hands looked more spotted, more frail than ever before. Grandpa wasn't going to be around forever...

Junker, Sr., pinned Junker, Jr., with a penetrating stare. "So what do you think happened to your friend Mr. Stipes yesterday?"

Anna's father sighed. "He was one of my patients, Dad. I was treating him for heart disease."

"With digitalis?"

"Yep."

"Tincture or tablets?"

"Tablets from the powdered leaves—the usual preparation. He was supposed to take them regularly, with meals. But sometimes he forgot. If he doubled up on a dose..."

"Or someone gave him an extra one..." Grandpa said, leaning back in the wing chair and emitting a big puff of fragrant smoke.

Junker and Anna both stared at him.

"But that would be murder, Grandpa!"

"Yep. Didn't you tell me, Illinois, that your pal Stipes was a reporter who liked to make people mad by digging around in unsavory areas? Maybe he made an enemy and that person found a way to give him something a little extra in his tonic bottle."

"Dad! I've no cause to think Stipes was deliberately poisoned! It's much more likely he overdosed by accident..."

"How, Grandpa?" asked Anna. "How could someone give him extra without his knowing about it?"

"I have no idea," Grandpa said. "Just thought I'd mention the possibility. You know how I like to play Devil's Advocate."

Junker glanced dubiously at Anna. "Wait, Dad. This is pure speculation, and neither of you can discuss this with anyone else! Anna, I am not happy that you are part of this!"

"Papa, I know it's unpleasant, but I *am* a nursing student. And," she added with a wicked little grin, "You know I've been helpful in your other cases..."

"And, so far, you have kept your trap shut. Right, then." Doc Junker rose and paced in front of the fire. "Just for the sake of argument, let's explore this. We have four possibilities: one, a natural heart attack with some unusual symptoms. Two, an accidental overdose, with Stipes taking more of his prescription tablets than he should have. Three, he drank something toxic, like one of those darn tonics, on top of his tablets and there was some kind of interaction. Four—the least likely, in my opinion—someone added something to either the flask he was carrying, or something he drank at another gin mill before I met him at seven. Adding the other form of medicine—digitalis as a tincture—to a drink would do the trick. He wouldn't notice the taste if he was drinking his usual white lightning."

"What are the symptoms of digitalis overdose, Papa?"

"Nausea, blurred vision, headache, vomiting...all heart symptoms as well. But the odd thing was that he complained of yellow vision."

"Xanthopsia?" Grandpa asked.

"Yep, I think so."

"But if he had a poisoned drink before he met you, Papa, it would be difficult to trace," said Anna.

Grandpa spoke up. "So get the flask tested!"

"I already have. I sent the bottle to a chemist, Jack Searles, over at the University. Should get results in a few days. I was hoping to arrange an autopsy as well, but Harry's wife refused permission."

Just before lunchtime, Anna decided to do some shopping. She needed silk stockings and a new shirtwaist, so she whizzed through Robeson's Ready-to-Wear department. Since she knew exactly what she wanted, it didn't take long.

Grateful to be on her own for once (no Sally to act like a magnet for fellas), Anna planned to have a sandwich and ice cream soda at Vriner's. She also wanted to gloat over her new friendship with Ben. They'd had such a nice time, sipping hot chocolate in the cozy kitchen and talking about themselves. She'd learned more about Ben Keck in half an hour than in the past eighteen years (her family had moved into the house when she was barely walking).

The way Ben looked at her gave her hope. He really knew how to focus on a girl, make her feel special. But his manner towards Anna was especially...interested. Maybe he liked Anna better than Sally. Maybe Ben hadn't initiated that kiss with Sally. Maybe he was more kissed against than kisser.

Sally never let another girl's feelings stop her from flirting—even if the other girl was supposed to be her best friend.

What if Sally sensed you were interested in Ben and kissed him deliberately?

Maybe Anna should cultivate new friends. Perhaps, if she had enough gumption, she could make Ben forget all about Sally McKinley. All the way down Main St., Anna carried on a scintillating, imaginary conversation about photography, painting, and books with Ben.

Anna arrived at Vriner's Confectionary at twelve-thirty, right in the middle of a busy lunch hour. The joint was smoky, noisy, and packed with secretaries and department store clerks. She was lucky to grab one of the last two stools at the marble-topped counter. She'd just ordered a ham-and-cheese-on rye and a chocolate soda when the door swung in and a cold breeze blew in Ben Keck.

He saw her right away. While she was still struggling to reconcile her daydream with sudden reality, he strode up to the counter and took the last empty stool next to her.

"Hi, Anna. Hope you don't mind if I join you." He took off his wool cap and shoved it into his pocket.

"Hello, Ben. Of course you can sit here—I mean...it's the last seat and everything." Anna hoped she wasn't blushing. At least she knew she looked fetching—she was wearing her midnight blue chemise that brought out the color of her eyes. And her cloche hat matched.

The waiter plunked down Anna's sandwich and soda and shoved a menu at Ben.

"I'll have what she's having," said Ben. He turned towards her with a shy grin. "I'm glad I ran into you, Anna. We didn't talk about Frank's behavior last night, and I wanted to apologize for him."

"Frank? Oh, at the Steamroom, you mean. When he was making a beeline for Sally and I was right in the way. He's a friend of yours, right?" She admired Ben's brown curls, neatly slicked back like Rudolph Valentino. He was wearing Oxford bags and a navy blue cardigan that darkened his eyes.

"Yep. We go back to grade school. I sat next to him in Mrs. Thompson's first grade class at Old Greg."

He meant Old Gregory Public School on Columbia St. "I

must have been right next door, in Miss Reid's class," Anna said, relieved that she'd found something to talk about.

Ben's sandwich arrived and he took a large bite. "Frank shares my interest in photography. He's been over to my darkroom several times, helped me process negatives."

"Where is your darkroom?" Anna asked.

"Dad lets me use the basement bathroom. It was easy to seal the edges around the door with tape and make it really black inside. I have a dark light, a platform for the enlarger that fits over the sink, a portable shelf that fits over the toilet for my trays—it's really slick. You should come see it sometime." His smile grew suddenly more intimate.

"Sure, I'd like that." Anna shivered a little from anticipation. "Do you and Frank do other things together?"

"He's a local history buff—he takes me around Champaign County and tells me stories about which buildings were here twenty years ago, which streets were paved when, stuff like that. And sometimes we go fishing together, out near his family's farm."

"Must be nice to have a friend like that," Anna said wistfully. "I mean someone you share interests with. Sally—all she wants to do is chase men and go to speakeasies."

"That doesn't surprise me at all."

"I have other friends, of course. But recently, it seems that they've all paired off and don't have time for just girl outings."

Ben gave her a shrewd look. "There's another side to friendship, you know."

"What do you mean?"

"Worrying about friends when they go do something stupid, or spend time with the wrong people. Take Frank. I'm worried about him," He swallowed the last bite of his sandwich and wiped his mouth with his sleeve.

"Because he drinks too much?" Anna asked.

"And combines it with coke, which is dangerous," Ben said with a scowl.

Anna remembered how Frank's eyes had bulged oddly, and wondered if cocaine did that. She was no expert, but any nursing student worth her salt knew that combining liquor and cocaine was bad news.

"What's he do with himself when he's not with you or boozing and doping at the speaks?" Anna asked, draining her chocolate soda with a long, satisfying slurp on the straw.

"He works for his uncle Big Bruce who runs the blacksmith and the speakeasy next door, and does odds and ends for his father."

"He hardly looks strong enough to be a blacksmith," observed Anna. Her glance followed a piece of chocolate cake that a waitress was carrying to a nearby table.

Ben noticed and raised his hand. "Yeah, he has kind of a weedy physique. I think he keeps accounts, takes orders, and runs errands for his uncle—picking up smokes and booze for the bar, that sort of thing. But it's not what he drinks and inhales that worries me."

The waitress appeared at Ben's side and he ordered two pieces of chocolate cake.

Anna felt a warm glow—party because he'd noticed she wanted the cake, but also because he was confiding in her. She shifted her knees under the counter so she was closer to him and lowered her voice. "What, then?"

Ben hitched his stool closer to Anna. "He's spending too much time with the Tate brothers, who are always up to no good, and a couple of other seedy types I've never seen before in this town."

Anna thought about what she'd do if Sally behaved that way. Of course, she was always dallying with unsuitable men— and going off with them in automobiles to places where Anna couldn't and didn't want to pursue her. "Can you distract him? Get him interested in something else? Lure him away to play billiards or something?"

"I wish," said Ben gloomily. "The thing is..." He looked around to make sure that everyone near them was involved in their own conversations. "...He keeps disappearing at night and won't tell me where he's been. And recently, he has more cash to throw around—he shows off, pulling a wad of bills out of his pocket every time he pays for something. I think he's involved in something criminal. He's going to get himself hurt, maybe worse. And I don't know any way to stop him."

Chapter Six

Most weeks, Doc Junker crisscrossed Champaign County several times, visiting everything from rural homes with big-sky views to urban fraternities in their bustling university community. He loved the contrasts: placid cows crossing muddy fields one moment, fur-coated co-eds flagging down the local popcorn truck the next. He and Martha both enjoyed the variety of living in such a place. You could watch Red Grange race down the football field, hear a fine concert in a university professor's home, or take in a lecture by a world-famous expert on campus.

Over the next few days, he delivered a breach birth over on White Street and twins at Burnham Hospital, visited a child with scarlet fever and another with whooping cough, and made a house call to a polio patient to measure his withered left leg for a new brace. On Tuesday, he reluctantly put Geoff Garwood, a patient who'd consumed too much Indiana moonshine, in the hospital to dry out. And of course, he held clinic hours from two to five in his surgery on Elm Boulevard every weekday except Wednesday.

Much of Junker's business these days had to do with over-consumption of bad booze. Before Prohibition, his patients drank, but the stuff they drank was usually legal and the ingredients were at least partially regulated. Now anyone could make bathtub gin with a miniature still purchased for seven bucks or get some quack to write him a prescription for pure alcohol. It was all the fault of the 1920 Prohibition law—a law that made it illegal to sell or transport liquor, but not to drink it. How was that supposed to work? Human nature being what it is, everybody and his brother became a moonshiner, and the coffin varnish they produced ranged from tolerable tasting and somewhat intoxicating to horrible and seriously toxic.

On Friday, his last clinic visitor was Eli Weaver who ran the garage over on Main Street. Eli was sixty-seven, skinny as a weathered fence post and almost as bald.

"Hello, Eli, how are you today?" He looked terrible, as if he hadn't slept recently.

"Not too bad, not too bad. But my fingers feel funny. I keep losing my grip on things."

Eli tap-clicked across the floor to the patient's chair, the front part of his foot dangling from the ankle so he couldn't walk normally. The toes hit first, and then the heels slammed down, jarring his whole skinny frame.

Watching him, Junker's heart sank. Eli was worse, much worse. Doc Junker knew he had Jake Foot—a peculiar affliction from drinking almost pure alcohol flavored with Jamaican ginger. Jake was legal—you could buy it at any pharmacy—but it was also the scariest stuff he'd ever encountered.

Doc Junker gave Eli his usual speech about laying off the hooch, or at least switching to something milder, noting that he was showing signs of paralysis in his fingers as well as his foot muscles. "Your symptoms will get worse, you know. That panther piss you're drinking is pure poison." He'd said all this to Eli a few weeks ago, but clearly he hadn't gotten through. Junker sighed. "And you ought to eat better than all those gin mill snacks. Get some meat and potatoes and vegetables, not just crackers and nuts."

"Whaal, Doc Junker, if I didn't drink, I wouldn't have much to live for. And if I didn't eat something at the speak, I'd probably forget to eat at all. Since my wife passed on last year, I just don't give a damn anymore."

Even when Karen had been alive, Eli had been as stubborn as Martha, which was saying something.

Something prompted Junker to ask, "What drugstore meds

are you taking now, Eli?"

"Whaal, nothin' much, just this tonic with vitamins my buddy Arnold likes so much. It's got a blue label..."

A blue label. Again! "Still got the bottle? I'd like to see what's in it."

"Maybe, Doc. I'll bring it by if I can find it."

Doc Junker asked Eli if he had enough cash, and he said he was okay for the moment. He had a small pension so he wasn't destitute, but he lived alone in the flat over the garage with no one to keep an eye on him. It was a dismal outlook; Junker didn't hold out much hope for him. Naturally, he didn't charge for the office visit. Martha would have something to say about that when she discovered it.

Eli tap-clicked his way out, and Junker took a break by opening his prized artifact cabinet. As always, the neat array of objects—pottery containers, a copper celt, stone projectile points, and pipe bowls—from other peoples' lives both fascinated and soothed him. His interest had only increased after the discovery of the pharaoh Tutankhamun's tomb in Egypt the previous year. All amateur archaeologists now pictured themselves as Howard Carter, stumbling upon a fabulous cache, full of "wonderful things."

Illinois Junker picked up a pipe he'd found in northern Illinois. It had the figure of a beaver, exquisitely carved from soft, gray-green pipestone. He knew it was soft stone because he'd been able to scratch it on the underside with a penny, but what kind of stone was it? Junker was no geologist, but he wanted to know everything he could about the materials and manufacture of each piece. He turned the piece over, admiring the smooth polish on the pipe platform and picturing a long stem added to the pipe bowl next to the beaver's tail. Had the craftsman used local stone, or carted it in from somewhere else? Was pipe-making a family activity, or part of a larger industry? So many questions.

Herself bustled into the surgery to do a little cleaning. While dusting the blinds, she exchanged family news and gossip with Junker.

"I get a letter today from Uncle Conrad out in Texas and do

you know what his youngest son Frederick did?"

"No, but I can imagine." Junker remembered Frederick as a lively lad, stubborn as all get out. He closed the case file on Eli and slipped it into the drawer.

"He refused to say his catechism at Sunday school and the pastor sends him home with his chair!" Martha's face turned dusky pink. "That is like being excommunicated in a Catholic church—the family is so upset, especially since Frederick is on the verge of being confirmed.

"Sounds like maybe Frederick doesn't want to be a Lutheran."

"Ach, Earl, you never seriously understand these things! Conrad's friend, the Methodist minister next door, offers to take Frederick in his church. That will mean the whole family becomes Methodist!"

Junker reflected that worse things could happen than being kicked out of church—he hardly ever attended the Lutheran church in town unless Martha nagged him. He was a Christmas and Easter churchgoer at best, and he saw no difference between the Methodist and Lutheran houses of worship. He debated what he could say that wouldn't inflame his wife further.

"Well, can't Conrad and his family check out the new church before they commit themselves?"

Martha just looked at him. Then she shook out her duster and changed the subject to their youngest son, Franz. "...he is not getting better, Earl. He hasn't been back to school in a week and I fear he is falling behind...I give him the medicine and tonic four times a day..."

Junker wasn't listening very closely because he was rummaging in his black bag and sorting out what needed cleaning. He'd checked Franz just that morning, and while he didn't like his son's pallor, he'd found nothing new to worry about.

In the meantime, Martha had switched to Anna and her brother Hans' latest fight, and then how Anna didn't spend enough time at home studying.

"...she doesn't concentrate on her work. How she will ever

graduate from nursing school, I do not know. Either she spends all her time getting ready to go out or reading those pulp magazines full of detective stories. She keeps burying her nose that *Argosy Weekly* instead of doing her chores. That girl is acting more feather-brained than usual. Her moods are so odd I am thinking she maybe fall in love…"

Junker grinned as he dropped his used instruments in a tray of boiling water. He knew about Anna's pulp magazines because he'd got her started reading them. Only he preferred *Black Mask* or *Adventure*, and he especially loved the science fiction stories of Edgar Rice Burroughs. The ones set on Mars were especially satisfying…He made an effort to keep up with his wife. "And why shouldn't Anna fall in love? You were almost married when you were her age."

"Bah! Being engaged did not stop me from book-learning," said his wife, who'd been at the top of her class at Burnham School of Nursing.

"Well, perhaps having a baby on the way steadied you…gave you a sense of urgency," Junker said.

She threw the duster at him. "And whose fault is that? She is not in my footsteps following, *Lieber Gott*. I will make sure of that." Martha's verbs wandered as her voice rose. "But she spends too much time in the speakeasies and on the streets. We do not know her friends any more. And that little hussy Sally McKinley is a bad influence."

Junker plucked the sterilized instruments out of the hot water with tongs and laid them on a clean cloth. "She is old enough to choose her friends—and to fall in love, if she wants to…"

"What about all the booze she drinks? You know how I feel about alcohol in the family…"

Oh, yes, Junker knew. Martha's father, Hans Friedrich Huber, had died of alcoholism and his violent and erratic behavior had destroyed her childhood. She constantly harped on her husband's consumption—wouldn't allow anything except a small bottle of sherry for entertaining in the house. 'Course she didn't know about the bottle of bonded whiskey he kept in a high cupboard. And now she'd joined the Women's

Christian Temperance Union, an insufferable group of do-gooder ladies with more time on their hands than sense.

"...those speakeasies are bad places, with their illegal hooch and loose women and drunkards. What kind of environment is that for our daughter?"

Junker reflected that if Martha had ever visited a speakeasy, she'd realize it wasn't so terrible. Yes, there was an occasional fight or unsavory character, but half the town's policemen, doctors, and lawyers haunted the speaks. He threw more fuel on the fire. "I refuse to worry about Anna unless she shows signs of wanting to marry someone unsuitable."

"Oh!' cried Martha. "Sometimes I wish we live in the times when marriages were arranged by the parents! Then we would surely two years ago all this planned..."

Mixed tenses again, a sure sign of growing agitation in his dear wife.

"Let a little time pass, *Lieblinge*. I am sure Anna will sort herself out."

Martha snorted her disbelief and bustled out of the room.

Junker had to admit he enjoyed stirring her up because her skin became so rosy it made him think of her stretched out on their bed when they made love by firelight ...something that happened far too infrequently these days. It had to be an occasion when Martha wasn't exhausted from minding four children and all the housework, when she wasn't preoccupied by her extended family in Texas or the latest anti-immigrant slur on the radio. Novel thought: if he courted his own wife again, would he think about sex with other women any less? Probably not...

As he tidied his office for the next day's patients, his wandering mind returned to Nathan Donaldson and his new archaeological site on the Tate Farm. What else had he found? It must be pretty good stuff if he wouldn't boast about his trophies as usual. Was he keeping the artifacts at home in east Big Grove, or someplace downtown Junker didn't know about, such as his brother Bruce's smithy on North Walnut Street? And Nate's behavior was peculiar to say the least. They'd always had a gentlemanly rivalry in their archaeological ventures, so why start shooting at Junker now?

Doc Junker found it amusing that he and Nathan seemed to be carrying on a much older tradition—"gentlemen" archaeologists digging mounds, forming their own museums, and occasionally writing up their finds like Christopher Adams over in the Quincy area. Now Adams had been a really colorful character until his untimely death (he fell drunk into a creek and drowned). He had a fearful temper, threatened to shoot anyone who messed with his digs, and always insisted the press give him the limelight in any news coverage. Word was his wife was so thrilled when he passed away that she took all his papers out into their driveway and burned them.

Doc Junker closed up his medicine cabinet. He must find an opportunity to visit the Tate Farm again—at a different time of day so he could snoop around. The Cunninghams were out that way—Junker owed them a visit in their bereavement. A bereavement that felt like his own fault, even though he doubted anyone could have saved Elizabeth in those circumstances. Would Gerry shut the door in his face? Wouldn't blame him if he did—losing a beloved daughter had to be one of the worst things the world could throw at you.

Junker pulled out his watch chain. Only four-thirty, but it was getting dark. He would try and go Wednesday afternoon, right after lunch. Wednesday, a no-clinic day, was the only day he could get away early.

Gerald himself opened the door. He just stood there, his round face balanced on a torso that seemed caved in, diminished. Then he pushed his shoulders back and motioned Junker in. "Illinois. 'Bout time you came back."

Relief flooded Junker and he realized he'd been holding his breath. "I'd have come sooner, Gerry, but I thought you and Jo needed a little time…"

"Rubbish. I mean, of course we need time for the grieving, but everyone else and his sister has been out here to see us. Why not you and Martha?"

Jo, her graying hair escaping from its bun, rushed out of the kitchen and threw her arms around him. "He's right, Illinois.

We've missed you."

Junker patted her back, inhaling the delicate lily-of-the-valley perfume she wore and enjoying the feel of her breasts squashed against his chest. This wasn't helping him keep his libido fixed on Martha... He gently grasped Jo's arms and set her away from him. "We'll come out this weekend," he promised, looking into her pretty face and noting the new lines from grief etched around her eyes. "I hope you are taking care of yourself, Jo? You've had terrible time, I'm sure."

Jo's shapely lips quivered. "I can't deny it's been awful. Elizabeth was such a darling. But Gerry and Alice are propping me up, and my committees will keep me busy."

Junker nodded. "And your younger children still need you. Jo, would it be all right if I kidnapped Gerald for an hour or two? I want to investigate something out at Tate Farm."

Jo cast a loving look at her husband. "Go along, Gerry, you need a break."

Gerald Cunningham and Junker had a pleasant ramble over the Tate Farm, poking around the old buildings and walking along the creek. Gerry seemed unwilling to say any more about his grief, so they talked about Big Grove politics and the local School Board.

"...You'd think the mayor would want us to buy new books and lab equipment for high school science classes, but no, he wants us to raise money and turn over control of it to him."

"Can't blame him for that," Junker said.

"That's not the point!" cried Gerry. "Every single Board member has the children's best interests at heart and..."

"Hey, what's that?" A pile of metal half in, half out of the streambed caught Junker's eye.

"Exactly what you think it is, Illinois." Gerry stopped and surveyed the remains.

"How long would you say it's been since it was operational?"

"Well, let's see. The outside's all rusted, so that means they used sheet iron instead of copper. Probably cheated on the copper tubing for the condenser too, so whatever they made here tasted horrible."

"Sounds like you know a lot about how to make a still, Gerry." Junker teased. He pulled out his pipe and filled it with fragrant cherry tobacco—the same brand Thomas Junker used.

"Should do. My grandfather lived in Georgia for a time, and he learned all there is to know about making good corn whiskey, from where to situate the still to how to choose the right kind of sprouted corn and how to burn the smoke..."

"'Burn the smoke?'" Junker made his own puff of fragrant smoke.

"Re-circulate the smoke back into the firebox so it's almost invisible to excise agents."

"Aha! Did he use sugar?" Junker knew sugar increased the yield.

"No, he always said sugar diluted the 'real' flavor. He liked real coffin varnish..."

Something else snagged Junker's attention. "Hey!"

"Hey, what?" Gerry sounded a bit miffed at being interrupted.

"That post. Look carefully."

Gerry stared at a lopsided, decaying fence post in the ground on the wrong side of the water, right where the stream took a bend to the east. A little pile of fresh dirt surrounded it. His gaze scanned the ground for the next post. "The fence line has been moved!"

"Yep. And I bet I know why." Junker trotted upstream and Gerald followed, favoring his right knee.

They stopped at the site uncovered by Nathan Donaldson.

"See?" Junker said. "This is the burial that Nathan's been working on. He hoped I wouldn't find out where it was, and looks like he wanted to make it appear to be off the Tate property. Hmm, I wonder who owns the adjacent property to the north?"

"I can tell you that," Gerry chuckled. "His brother Big Bruce does."

"Well, well!" Junker said. "If I can prove it was Nathan who moved the posts, then I might have a chance to clean up this dig and make sure it's done properly."

"You don't fool me," Gerry said. "I can see the glint in your

50

eyes. You want some of those artifacts for your collection!"

"Who, me?" Junker smiled into his beard.

Chapter Seven
Thursday afternoon

Jo Cunningham picked up Martha Junker at her house on Elm Boulevard.

"Don't you look nice," Jo said, as she opened the door of her Pathfinder for Martha.

"Thank you. This is my new suit—I bought it only last week." It was wool tweed in a subtle green-and-gold plaid, with a dropped waist and a wide-lapelled coat that fastened with a single oversized button. With four children to outfit, Martha rarely bought new clothes for herself. She was delighted that Jo could take notice of new clothes despite her grief over the death of her daughter.

Both women wore felted hats with down-turned brims, seamed stockings, and pointy-toed shoes with low heels. A gathering of the Women's Christian Temperance Union demanded careful dressing and best behavior. The meeting itself always presented a delicious contrast: the serious business the slowing down or preventing the consumption of alcohol in any form, followed by the giddy pleasure of the social hour where the ladies gossiped and caught up with their friends.

Jo, as president of the local chapter, had secured the upper meeting room at the Athenaeum, which also housed the public library. It was a spacious room with a high ceiling, a hardwood floor, and floor-to-ceiling windows.

They arrived in a bustle of women greeting each other and shedding their long winter coats.

They were engulfed in a sea of hellos and how-are-yous.

Martha watched her friend behave with dignity and grace, admiring how well she functioned in the midst of her deep sorrow. Running the show was probably a welcome distraction for Jo.

"Ladies! Let's be seated and begin our meeting. We have important business today." Jo moved to the podium bearing a sheaf of notes and adjusted her spectacles.

Martha settled in the second row, next to Cora Busey and Gretchen McKinley. Both Cora and Gretchen were overdressed, sporting too much lipstick and wearing low-cut chemises and pearls under their sweaters that looked more suitable for evening wear. Like mother, like daughter, thought Martha sourly as she remembered her last glimpse of Gretchen's daughter Sally McKinley. Or maybe Gretchen was pretending she was a flapper...

Jo Cunningham moved briskly through minutes, old business, the treasurer's report, and plans for the next fundraiser. "Now ladies, I have an idea I'd like to propose to you. We are gathered here because of our common abhorrence of liquor and its effects on our menfolk and our youngsters who are spending far too much time at local speakeasies..."

"Hear, hear!" said Martha, who spent many nights lying awake plotting how to get Anna and Earl to stop, or at least curtail, their drinking. She knew all about the bottle of whiskey in the high cupboard in the kitchen that her husband believed was a secret. Martha hated the fact that Earl drank whiskey, just like her father. Well, not just like: Earl savored his whiskey in small amounts, but her father had swilled it by the bucketful. But her husband had those nightmares about the war...he could get sucked in to heavier drinking...

"Our posters, pamphlets, and education sessions have produced few results. I think it is time for more drastic action." Jo paused, gathering up the audience's attention with her flashing eyes and proud stance at the podium. Martha thought she looked magnificent.

"We'll take the fight to the enemy. Let us plant some of our own members in the speakeasies to collect solid evidence of illegal activity, and then see how many speakeasies and blind pigs we can shut down!"

The meeting exploded into a cacophony of sixty-five female voices. Everyone had an opinion.

"Brilliant idea!" cried a woman at the back of the room.

Martha said, "But who would go work in a blind pig? It's not decent! And the national WCTU would not approve!" Nor would the local chapter of the Ku Klux Klan—if they found out about it.

"No daughter of mine will take a job like that!" said Gretchen McKinley.

Gretchen obviously had no idea what her daughter Sally was up to, thought Martha. She'd always thought it ironic that so many of the women preached temperance for other families but ignored the fact that their own teenagers and husbands drank like fish. Carrie Nation would probably ban such loose-minded women from WCTU membership.

"What kind of proof do we need? Everyone knows all these places sell bootleg whiskey and gin..."

"But would it work?" asked another woman.

Jo waited for the hubbub to die down. "This is not a totally new idea," she said. "One of our younger members proposed it a few weeks ago, and we've been working out the details. And yes, the national organization will approve our effort if we actually manage to close down some illegal liquor distribution hubs. Karin, would you come up front?"

A tall young woman in her late twenties glided to the podium. She was neatly and soberly dressed, with her brown hair neatly bobbed a bit longer than was fashionable.

"My name is Karin Keillor. I come from Sweden originally, and my papa was an alcoholic. He beat my mother and my brother, so bad that Neil and I ran away from home. At age sixteen I come to America, with Neil. We were not accepted— we were shunned because we were immigrants..."

Martha felt immediate sympathy for the young woman. She herself knew exactly what it felt like to arrive in a new country as a teenager with poor English and no skills. Her father had settled in Chicago while his brother Conrad journeyed to Fredericksburg, Texas. The four cousins who'd grown up together were separated for the first time in their short lives, and Martha found it terribly hard to make new friends. The kids in her Chicago neighborhood were suspicious of her because of their parent's distrust of foreigners.

Getting married hadn't helped. Junker was a common German name, and anything German was reviled during the Great War. Only a few years ago, right after the lynching of German immigrant Robert Prager in Collinsville, Illinois, Martha and her husband had seriously considered changing their last name to Jones. The only thing that stopped them was Earl's fear that his patients would find the name change too confusing... Ach! Time to pay attention to Karin's speech.

"...And so with the help of you wonderful ladies, we finally had jobs. I would like to help this organization that has given me so much friendship and assistance." Karin took a sip of water and cleared her throat.

Martha reflected that Karin was lucky to belong to the WCTU at all—immigrants were not automatically accepted into the local chapter unless senior members vetted them. An immigrant had to be religious, preferably Protestant, and demonstrate commitment to an alcohol-free life. She herself had been admitted only after Jo Cunningham vouched for her.

"My brother Neil now works at a blind pig called the Cat's Pajamas on Randolph Street. He says his employer is looking for a server, and he knows other joints that are short-handed. If we could have a few more volunteers—I have five already—we would have a team that could take jobs serving set-ups and drinks..."

Cora Busey objected. "But how would this help? The federal agents know where most of these places are already."

"Not all of them," Jo said with a thin smile. "We have at least twenty-five speakeasies, blind pigs, roadhouses, and restaurants serving liquor in Champaign County."

Karin continued. "Our servers could watch for hard proof, like receipts from distributors, labels off bottles, that sort of thing."

"And steal them?" asked Martha. Despite herself, she felt a thrill at the idea of doing something so contrary to her strict

Lutheran upbringing.

"Yes."

The ladies reacted vociferously.

"But stealing's against the law!"

"Not if you're collecting evidence for excise agents."

"What if someone gets caught?"

"Then she gets fired," said Jo. "But she won't be out of pocket because I propose we pay these young women a fee and expenses out of our treasury."

More discussion. Martha didn't like the idea when she thought of her Anna behind a bar—or worse, serving drinks to older men who would leer at her and pinch her bottom—but she had to agree the scheme might produce results.

At least it would for the women who were willing to buck society's norms and volunteer as barmaids. That certainly didn't include Martha....

Late again. Anna was supposed to meet Ben in twenty minutes, and she hadn't even decided what to wear. Shoes flew left and right as Anna rooted through her closet searching for her favorite pair of boots, the ones that had a convenient loose top for her pewter flask. Drat it, where were they?

She was dressed only in a white camisole and knickers. Two pairs of silk stockings, one Honey Beige plain and one Rose Morn with a diamond pattern, festooned her chair while three dresses in totally different styles were laid out on the bed.

Muttering, Anna finally pulled out her brown leather boots and black patent leather Mary Janes with two-inch heels and diamante buckles.

Her sixteen-year-old brother stuck his head in the room. "Getting on your glad rags again?"

Anna straightened. "Hans! Don't sneak up on me like that!"

Hans laughed. "I wasn't sneaking. You just had shoes on the brain. Personally, I think you look fine the way you are." He looked her up and down. "Maybe add a rope or two of pearls?"

She threw a shoe at him and he vanished. Anna returned to the closest and began the same procedure with dresses and accessories. Soon the bed behind her was piled high with possible garments.

Martha Huber Junker entered the room with a pile of folded sheets and towels just as Anna was standing, stork-like, on one leg vacillating between the beige, drop-waisted dress (to wear with the boots and brown tasseled hat) or the black jersey with fake flower and the Mary Janes.

Uh oh, her mother was still dressed up from her afternoon at the Women's Christian Temperance Union meeting with Jo Cunningham. That probably meant she was in a Temperance mood and Anna was due for a lecture. Of course, her mother didn't wear flapper fashions, but sober long skirts and long-sleeved blouses or twinsets. And instead of a short bob, Martha wore her hair long, pinned back in a neat bun or with the braid wrapped round her head like a crown.

Maybe she could fend off the inevitable with a distraction. Anna picked up the *Sears Catalogue* she'd found in the upstairs bathroom with a page turned down over a very interesting set of item under the heading "AIDS THAT EVERY WOMAN APPRECIATES." It showed ads (and pictures) of everything from fans, room heaters, and eggbeaters to home motors with attachments. One of the attachments was a vibrator. Anna knew what the vibrator was for—it was actually labeled "very useful and satisfactory for home service." Of course she'd discussed it with Sally, but she was dying to see what her mother's reaction was to her new knowledge.

"Mama, I didn't know you were interested in these!" Anna said with a tiny giggle.

Her mother glanced at the page and blushed. "Give me that!"

"Don't worry, Mama, I know all about it." Then she realized that comment was probably unwise.

It was. "And how would you, an unmarried girl, know anything about such devices?"

Anna omitted the discussion with Sally. "I read, Mother, and I go to movies. You can't avoid finding out things if you pay any attention at all. So, are you going to order one?"

"Anna!"

"I'll never tell."

"Actually, I was interested in the electric heater."

"Sure you were, Mama!"

Martha shook her head and opened her mouth. "Anna, I really don't want you to..."

Anna changed the subject quickly. "Mama, what do you think?" Anna asked, holding up the sleeveless black dress against her slender torso.

"It's too low-cut. Wear the beige, it's modest, and more becoming to your coloring." Martha dumped the sheets on Anna's bed and sat down on the end of it. "And maybe you could tone down the makeup, for once, instead of looking like a vampire with those blood-red lips?"

Anna giggled. "You think my lipstick is red, you should see what Sally wears. Hers is so dark it looks like dried blood, kind of a purplish-black." She'd been leaning towards the black dress, but it was easier to pacify her mother in the room if she wore the beige. But that meant patterned stockings to liven up her outfit, and a few ropes of fake pearls around her neck.

Martha said, "Anna, I do hope you are not drinking alcohol when you go out. It is so unladylike, and my friends at the WCTU say..."

"Mama, I have an occasional drink, but it's not whiskey, mostly fruit juice." She had no intention of describing just how many different things could be mixed with that fruit juice. "And I know when to stop, so never mind what you and your temperance friends say."

"Fruit juice disguises the taste, and who knows how much hooch goes into the glass first! Besides, going to a speakeasy in bad company puts you. And that Sally is such a flirt..."

"Mo-uh-ther! Sally is my friend, and besides, I don't copy her behavior." Not much, anyway. And Anna didn't copy Sally's mode of dress, either. She could just imagine the way her mother's eyes would bulge if she saw Sally's favorite bustier sleeveless vest: it made her bubs rise as if they were being served up on a platter.

"At least pick a quiet place tonight, where there will not be any fighting."

Anna struggled both to control her irritation with her mother and to roll her stockings up without catching the silk on her fingernails. Later, when the dancing started, she'd roll them down part way. "Mother, all the speakeasies have fights occasionally. But I know how to stand out of the way, and Tommy or Ben is usually there to act as protector..."

"Ben? Ben who?"

"Ben Keck, Mama. You know, the boy next door." Anna felt herself blushing. She reached for her puff to powder her stockinged legs.

Her mother pounced. "Anna Maria! You're not falling in love with the Keck boy, are you? He's too young for you!"

"I don't know about falling in love, Mama, but I am seeing him. And he's twenty-one this month."

"But there are such nice young men, a little older, established like Heinrich Fritz, or Joseph Mattis. You need a doctor, a lawyer, someone who a home for you can make." Martha looked at her daughter's powdered legs. "And I do not see why you do that, dirtying good silk stockings."

Good grief, how many times had she heard this? Anna took a deep breath. "Mama, I already told you, it's the fashion to tone down the shininess of the stockings with powder." She picked up the long, wraparound coat with the diamante buckle and stooped so she could adjust her brimmed hat in the mirror. "Now, I've no interest in Heinrich or Joseph, even though you keep inviting them to dinner like I was dessert or something. They're all thirty-something, practically old men! Besides, I *like* Ben Keck!"

"Ach! You stubborn child! I am only thinking of what is best for you."

"I know that. But don't rush me. I don't want to think about marriage until I have my nursing degree and some work experience. You keep saying you want me to be able to support myself, but how can I do that if I marry as early as you and Father did?"

"Well, things were different in our day."

Sure they were.

Anna picked up her fringed purse, already loaded with her flask, money, and house key. "I'm going now, Mother. I won't be out very late tonight."

Martha rose from the bed. "Later than you should be, I think..." She trudged down the hall.

Chapter Eight
Friday

By the next evening, Martha had stopped worrying about Anna's late nights and was swallowed by another domestic problem. She was waiting for Earl to come home so they could talk about Franz.

Martha's nursing training and herbalist skills were sufficient to deal with most common ailments. Her garden out back produced peppermint and ginger root that she made into teas for upset tummies, as well as other medicinal herbs (anise seed for congestion, tansy for skin infections) that she dried and stored in her pantry. But this time, the nausea and loose stools that had plagued her youngest twin for two weeks now were not abating. Just an hour ago the little boy had exploded into violence. When she gave him his suppertime doses of bismuth and tonic, Franz thrashed and kicked. One kick landed on her stomach, winding her.

"Franz! You must not kick your mother!"

The boy looked right past her and yelled, "I don't want it! I don't want it! Let me go." He seemed suddenly as strong as his older brother, Hans.

She grabbed his face with both hands. "Franz! Look at me!"

He stared uncomprehendingly. "Mother! Mother!" he called, as if she were not even there. Then his arms and legs gyrated out of control, like a baby having a screaming fit.

Martha was scared for the first time. She gathered him into her strong arms and rocked him until he calmed down enough to take his medicine.

After Franz drifted back to sleep, Martha fixed herself a scratch supper of leftover bratwurst and pickled red cabbage. She sat down at the kitchen table, feeling exhausted and out of her depth.

Martha was accustomed to long hours in the house alone with the children. But this was one time when she really wished Earl would get home earlier so they could have a proper chat. He'd been so rushed lately, driving all over the county for childbirths and farm accidents, that she hardly ever saw him between early morning and late at night.

She glanced at the clock. Nine-fifteen: Anna and Hans were out, naturally, Emma was in bed, and Grandpa had retreated to his bedroom. Martha listened to the tick-tock of her German clock, normally a comforting sound. Tonight, it got on her nerves.

The front door lock squeaked as someone inserted a key.

"I'm home!" called Junker.

Martha met him in the hall. "Have you eaten? I have some cabbage and bratwurst to heat up."

"I don't need anything," her husband said, patting his gut. "Every patient I visited today insisted I taste something. Mary Lund gave me bread to bring home." He thrust a fragrant, newly-baked loaf into her hands.

"Mmm! Mary makes the best bread; I put it away for tomorrow." She stowed the loaf in the white-and-black breadbox on the counter. "Earl, I worry about Franz. He is no better and he had some strange behaviors tonight."

Junker followed her upstairs. On the way to Franz's room, he pushed the door to their bedroom open to check on Emma. They'd moved a trundle bed in there so Franz's nighttime bouts of sickness wouldn't wake his twin sister. Emma was sprawled half out of her covers, blond curls tumbled, and her favorite doll on the pillow. Junker scooted her legs under the quilt and pulled the covers up over her thin shoulders.

They entered the twins' room.

Franz lay still without any of the muttering and thrashing that had recently characterized his sleep.

Junker crossed to his son's bed and touched the boy's

forehead, smoothing back the blond curls. Whipping out his stethoscope, he listened to Franz's chest. "What in tarnation...he's unconscious!" said Junker. His voice shook slightly. "How long has he been like this?"

Martha's knees wobbled under her. She sat on edge the bed and took one of Franz's clammy hands in her own. "Not long. It can't be long...I left him barely an hour ago and he was just calming down after that craziness I tell you about. When he kicked me."

"I don't understand," Junker muttered into his beard. He reviewed Franz's symptoms out loud. "Nausea on and off for several days, loose stools for about a week before that, now agitation and losing consciousness. If I didn't know better, I'd think he were drugged. There's nothing in his medicine that would do this...he's had pink bismuth and a light diet." He sat back and let the stethoscope fall. Then he turned to Martha. "*Lieblinge*, he's had nothing except your herbal teas and the medicine I prescribed, right?"

Martha met his gaze with wide eyes and trembling lips. Her own stomach descended through the floor to the living room below.

"*Martha!* What have you been giving him?" Junker grabbed her arm.

"Earl, don't! You hurt my arm!" she snatched it back from him and rubbed the forearm. "It's a cureall...a tonic. The same one Jo Cunningham used when her youngest had the stomachache for so long. She says it worked..."

Junker paled and his mouth thinned to a line. "Show me the bottle."

She left the room and returned a few minutes later with a squat, blue bottle.

Junker grabbed it from her hand and stared at it. The label sported the now familiar Big Blue Stem grasses and the name "Blue Fire Stomach Aid: Good for Indigestion, Constipation, Nausea, Ulcers...Take One Tablespoon Four Times a Day as long as Symptoms Persist..." He groaned. "Another quack remedy. Martha, how could you? God only knows what's in here!" He took his son's pulse. "No time to waste; call the ambulance."

Martha, her heart thudding against her chest wall, ran to the phone. She dropped the receiver in her haste. Forcing her trembling finger to dial, she concentrated on getting the number right.

In fifteen minutes, the ambulance had arrived and the medics were loading Franz onto a stretcher.

Martha and Junker followed the ambulance to Burnham Hospital. She could barely contain herself in the car. Anger fought with fear; she was furious with her husband for questioning her judgment and scared to death about her son. Martha could feel the thunderclouds building in her head—if she weren't very careful, she'd say something unforgivable.

"Earl—I know I should have asked you about the tonic. But you are so busy lately."

He growled. "Not now, for heaven's sake! Let's get the boy seen to then we'll talk."

Martha closed her mouth, knowing he was right.

In short order, Junker parked the Tin Lizzie and they hustled inside the hospital to the admissions desk. Junker reminded the head nurse that he was one of the physicians on staff and said his son needed immediate attention; fortunately there were no other urgent cases ahead of them, and the doctor on call was a close friend of his.

A nurse wheeled the gurney carrying Franz, still unnaturally pale and unconscious, into an alcove. Junker disappeared behind the curtain, leaving Martha to wait outside while her husband conferred with Dr. Throckmorton.

After what seemed like an eternity—probably only ten minutes—she lost control. Martha marched over to the curtain and pulled it aside.

"Earl, what's going on?" she wailed, hating herself for sounding so unprofessional, so much like a distraught mother.

Junker had the grace to look ashamed for abandoning her.

His colleague answered for him. "Your son has taken a drug overdose. It appears that the tonic you gave him had cocaine or something like cocaine in it—we won't know for sure until the tests come back. But we may be facing a case of addiction to the drug; he will have his stomach pumped, then he will have to be weaned off of it. That will take days, maybe weeks."

Martha gasped. "Cocaine! That is a bad drug! Oh, how is this possible?"

Dr. Throckmorton said, "Unfortunately, cocaine is added to far too many substances these days. Regulation of drugs is very spotty; there's hardly any enforcement of it. It is not your fault, ma'am. You couldn't have known."

Tears ran down Martha's face. "But I should have guessed! I am a nurse, married to a doctor!" She looked at her husband, and their glances locked briefly.

Then Junker turned back to his colleague. "Tell us what the treatment is for this addiction, if that is what it is, and we will follow your instructions. Does Franz need to remain in the hospital longer than overnight?"

"Several days of observation would be best. We will let him go home once his condition is stable."

The Junker household was turned inside out as the family adjusted to Franz's treatment for cocaine addiction. They took turns visiting him in the hospital, and Anna found her social life curtailed by extensive babysitting duties for her younger sister.

Martha and Junker had their showdown in the kitchen a few nights after Franz was hospitalized.

"Earl, I know I should not have given him the tonic, but you were away so much and I..."

"It's a necessity for my job, Martha, you know that!"

"So you pay more attention to your patients than to your own son!"

"Not fair, Martha! And I could say that, since you are a trained nurse, you should have been less gullible, more cautious! We don't fully understand drug interactions yet, but you've heard me talk about what happens when patients dose themselves with home remedies on top of prescription medicines..."

"But Jo said it was good medicine! It cured her child!"

" 'Medicine,' my left foot! Snake oil and toilet water, more likely!"

This comment made Martha so mad that she picked up a frying pan and hefted it while glaring at her husband. Then she picked up a bunch of bananas and threw that instead.

"Ow! You crazy woman! Throwing fruit won't change anything!"

Eventually the recriminations faded into tears and hugs. Junker apologized to Martha for being so distracted that he'd not paid proper attention to his youngest son. Martha promised not to throw any more kitchen items at him.

Gradually, Franz recovered. The seizures faded and his appetite returned. After six days in hospital, Dr. Throckmorton sent him home.

But Martha was profoundly shaken. She spent her days performing her usual tasks mechanically while her mind whirled and seethed, reviewing everything she'd ever believed about nursing, about marriage—and about booze. She lay awake at night remembering her father's complex relationship with alcohol and patent medicines. One moment Hans Friedrich would be gay and loving, playing with his children and promising them excursions.

"Come, I will swing you around the world!" And the children would line up, giggling, waiting for their turns to be swung high in an arc and then round and round.

"This weekend, I'll take you all to the circus!" he'd say, but that day never came because he'd start drinking. Then he'd imbibe one whiskey too many and stomp and rage around the house. One night he beat his wife and Martha witnessed it as she kept the younger children out of the way, afraid to intervene, unable to leave her siblings to run for help. Trust in her father flew out the window as she learned that his personality was weak, his behavior erratic, and his promises rarely kept.

She finally came to terms with another, more private fear: her abhorrence of liquor was partly due to the fact that she'd actually enjoyed getting tiddly a few times as a young woman. She'd loved how shandies and hard cider made her feel both elated and daring. But deep down, she was afraid that if she didn't keep a tight rein on herself, if she let go, she'd become like her father: dependent on the demon alcohol to lift her mood, unreliable and unloved.

One morning, Martha woke up determined to take some kind of action. And she remembered the WCTU project of sending women into the speakeasies to collect evidence of illegal hooch.

Maybe, just maybe, Martha could participate herself. Surely, one of the roadhouses on the edge of town would prefer a more mature, motherly looking woman to be a server. What better way to see what it was really like inside a speakeasy, where her daughter and her husband spent so much time? She shivered as the novel idea took over. Her mama would roll over in her grave...but her mama wasn't here anymore.

And she was not going to tell Earl. She was still angry with him for treating her like the lowest nursing student instead of an equal partner. Anna would have to know—she'd be babysitting her siblings while Martha was at work. And what about transportation? They had only one vehicle, the Model-T that Junker used to visit his patients.

Jo Cunningham was the only woman Martha knew who had her own car—the result of a surprise legacy that Jo had insisted on spending herself so she could transport herself to all her committee meetings. Jo would help her.

Chapter Nine
A few days after Thanksgiving

"What's the password?" The attendant held the wooden flap in the unmarked door open just enough so Anna could reply.

"'Now you're on the trolley,'" she replied.

The door swung wide.

The Steamroom was hopping, as usual. Sally, Steve, and the others were already holding court at the bar, which boasted a collection of dead soldiers at one end. Sally—dressed in a slick black skirt and the satin vest that cinched her waist and made her bubs bulge like grapefruit—waved at her as Anna looked around for a table. Good, there was a free one on the side, at the back.

It was Anna's first night out in a week after being pressed into babysitting her sister Emma while her parents looked after Franz. As much as she loved her family and rejoiced that Franz had recovered, she was glad to be released, to live her own life again.

Anna shed her coat and draped it over a chair as a placeholder. Then she teetered over to the bar, her Mary Janes clacking on the rough wooden floor, and ordered a cranberry sling without the gin.

"Oh, a hot tomato tonight!" someone called.

Steve nudged Ben Keck, who was next to him at the bar. "Give your little sheba some gin!"

"Oh, mind your potatoes!" Ben said. He slid off his high stool and came to meet Anna. "What are you drinking?"

"Just fruit juice tonight, Ben. I want to keep my wits about me." Anna smiled up at Ben, basking in the warm feeling of being greeted by someone she actually liked. She glanced over at the bar and caught Sally's amused expression. *Go ahead and laugh, Sally, Ben's with me now—and you know ab-so-lute-ly nothing about it 'cause I'm not talking.*

"Good-oh," Ben said, following her back to her table. "I wish I could say the same for Frank; he's on a toot."

"Doing hooch and coke again?" Anna asked as she sat down.

"I don't know. Look at him." Ben nodded at the corner table on the other side of the bar. "Whatever he's imbibing, he's well on his way to being ossified." He turned back to Anna. "You're looking pretty swell tonight."

Anna blushed. "Thanks, Ben." The glow on her face and neck traveled down to the pit of her stomach as he continued to gaze at her. He's not really handsome, she thought, but he sure is appealing with that wavy brown hair and hazel eyes. The way his mouth turned up at one corner when he smiled quickened her breath.

Then he amazed her. "You know, I really prefer the way you dress to Sally. She's so flamboyant, with that blood red lipstick and all."

Anna tried to be fair. "Well, bright red goes with her dark coloring."

"I prefer blondes." Ben said, and winked.

Hot dawg, he was flirting with her! She'd always thought Ben Keck was shy, but maybe not. She suspected she was entering the goofy stage about Ben and hoped it didn't show too much.

"Hey, look." Anna pointed to Frank's table. Frank's uncle Bruce Donaldson had arrived and was chatting with his nephew. As Anna and Ben watched, Frank pulled himself out of his slouch and shoved his glass to the far side of the table. Looked like he was trying to appear less spifflicated, but he shoved too hard and the glass slopped booze on table.

Ben frowned. "Big Bruce has a real hold over Frank. I don't quite know why."

"Isn't Bruce both his uncle and his employer?"

"Yes, but Frank is usually so casual about it. I wonder…"

"You wonder what they're up to?" Anna didn't know why she'd said that.

Ben gave her a sharp glance. "You're right. I'm uncomfortable about Frank, but I have no idea why. He's been different lately, sort of over-excited one moment and surly the next, and very cagey about his activities. We used to be close buddies, but now I have no idea what's going on inside his head…" He paused.

Anna's attention diverted to the short man in the corner. "Sorry, Ben. I'm listening, I really am, but I just spied Tommy Crouch—you know he's Father's assistant—over there, and he's truly zozzled. Look at him."

Ben turned his head and took in the sight of Tommy, slumped over his tiny round table, two empty glasses in front of him. "Wonder what he drinks? It seems to be affecting him rather strongly."

"Father says it's whiskey, but bad local stuff because he hoards his salary and won't shell out for decent booze. Probably made in a car radiator with all kinds of stuff added." She realized she was echoing her father's pet peeve: the manufacture of cheap alcohol that did far more harm than getting a person drunk. "Father asked me to keep an eye on Tommy. His drinking bouts are starting to affect his work."

"At least he sticks to one kind of hooch and doesn't appear to be mixing drinking with snorting coke, like Frank."

"True. I've never seen him drink anything but whiskey," Anna said.

Activity was picking up at Frank's table. His pal Dick Tate had joined him, and the two were engaged in an intense discussion with Big Bruce. His brother Nathan limped over, dragging his Thomas splint, and the conversation grew noisier. Bruce Donaldson made some point to the accompaniment of shouts of laughter, and then made his way to the door of the Steamroom, greeting patrons and shaking hands as he went.

Such a jolly fella, Anna thought cynically. But his eyes wander when he mentally undresses young women. And Papa is not friendly with him anymore.

"Don't look now," said Ben, grabbing Anna's wrist.

"What?"

"Frank and Dick are leaving, right after Big Bruce, for all they tried to make their departures look unconnected. I'm going to follow them." He drained his glass and stood

Anna turned toward the door and spotted Dick Tate supporting Frank, who had a tendency to weave. She surprised herself. "Take me with you, Ben."

"I don't know..."

"Two sets of eyes are better than one. I can help. Please."

Ben's sudden grin made her heart skip. "C'mon, then."

Ben's car was an older Model T Ford, borrowed from his Dad. With its peeling paint, dusty interior, and cigarette butts on the floor, it resembled a down-and-out rummy. The passenger seat was lumpy, and Anna shifted her behind to find a more comfortable position. She cast a covert glance at Ben as he pushed the electric starter on the floor of the automobile.

His profile showed a serious set to his mouth and hooded eyes. Ben was worried about his friend Frank and not paying much attention to her. She didn't really care where they were going; it was enough to be alone with Ben and part of his adventure.

As Ben smoothly navigated the recently paved streets of downtown Big Grove, Anna concluded that he was a good driver—a little fast, but nothing like the erratic and usually blotto Tommy Crouch. She always wondered if she was going to end up stuck to a tree whenever Tommy Crouch drove her home.

"Which car is Frank's?" she asked as they left the main road and headed out of town.

"That dark blue Model-T two cars ahead. It looks like only Frank and Dick—no Big Bruce. Maybe he's not part of this night errand." Ben said. "Hey, could you butt me? The lighter's in the compartment."

Anna found the lighter. She fished out a cigarette from the pack on the seat next to her and expertly lit it. She didn't smoke herself, but had plenty of practice lighting cigarettes for all her friends.

The paved road gave way to gravel as they turned south on Route 130. As the number of cars dwindled, Ben shut off his headlights so they wouldn't be spotted by Frank's car. Shivering a little, Anna cranked up the window against the freezing drizzle.

Ben shot her a grin as the road dipped and the car rumbled beneath them. "The shocks are gone on this bus. Dad doesn't maintain her very well. I'm going to get my own vehicle as soon as I have enough saved up...

"Look! He's turning off to the left," said Anna.

"Thanks. Here we go." He took the curve fast and gravel flew up and pelted the passenger side of the car.

Anna gripped the seat with both hands.

"Sorry," Ben said. "I don't want to lose them. This car is really reliable; don't worry."

"I'm not worrying," Anna said untruthfully. She was beginning to wonder what they would encounter when they caught up with Frank and Dick. And she knew darn well she was in for a lecture from her mother when she got home...if she got home. And with her brother still convalescent, she was expected to be available for babysitting, not take off to the other side of the county.

The car flashed by a wooden sign that read, "Tate Farm, 2 miles."

"Tate Farm!" Ben said with satisfaction. "I was right."

"Did you know Frank was heading there?"

"I guessed. He talks about some archaeological site he's digging out there with his father, but I can't believe that's the reason he's out here this late at night."

Anna saw the headlights of the car ahead of them dim. "They've stopped."

Ben picked up speed and passed the Tate Farm driveway. "I'll park down around the next curve, so they won't guess we followed them."

Anna suddenly realized her shoes were totally inappropriate for skulking around a farm at night. "Ben, my shoes..."

"I already thought of that. My kid brother's shoes are on the back seat—see if they fit your feet."

She twisted around and found muddy tennis shoes on the floor. When the car stopped, she grabbed them by the knotted laces and, after fumbling with the knots, slipped them on. A bit large, but certainly better than the Mary Janes for a farm trek.

Ben eased the car behind a handy bush near one of the outbuildings and turned off the ignition. He opened the door cautiously and motioned to Anna to slide over. She hopped out and he left the door slightly open instead of slamming it shut.

"Now what?" Anna said, wishing she'd brought a cardigan or at least a muffler as an extra layer. She turned up her coat collar.

"Follow me." Ben moved off with scarcely a rustle as if he'd been tailing people all his life.

Anna tried to be quiet, but the borrowed shoes made it difficult. They crept along the side of the building until they could see the main farmyard and the entrance to the barn. Frank and Dick stood at the side door, Frank leaning against the wall as if he needed support while Dick fiddled with a set of keys. The two men disappeared inside the barn, and soon Anna saw the glow of a kerosene lantern.

"Let's sneak up to that window and see what's going on," Ben said, gesturing at a small window on the left side of the main door. Without waiting to see if Anna followed him, he strode forward.

Anna held back, grateful that the drizzle had slowed and was no longer sliding down her neck and leaving icy trails inside her coat collar. Whatever Dick and Frank were up to, it was clear from the way they looked around before they entered the barn that they were up to No Good.

Ben reached the window. Cautiously, he peeked in. Then he motioned to Anna to join him. His hair was slicked with rain but his eyes were bright with excitement.

"See? There are two rooms at least. I'm going to try and break into the back," he whispered.

"Surely not when they can hear you?" Anna said.

"No, we'll wait until they leave." He took Anna's arm and led her to a dry spot under a large pine tree. They waited.

After about fifteen minutes, the two men exited the barn, locked the door, and took off in the battered Ford.

Ben snuck around the back of the building. Anna stayed put, watching for any strange movements and shivering. The sky above her cleared, showing stars around the edges of a massive dark cloud, and a cold breeze picked up. She stomped her feet up and down, trying to get warm.

Then she heard rustling and snapping sounds. Like something heavy rolling over dead leaves and twigs. Whirling around, Anna saw the battered Ford returning—without lights.

That could only meant that she and Ben had been spotted and that the two men were coming back to nail them.

Hugging the bushes between her and the access road, Anna sprinted to the back of the barn where Ben had disappeared.

"Ben! Get out of there! They're coming back!"

Ben reappeared empty-handed and ran past her, leading the way behind yet another outbuilding. She followed, discovering that she could run much faster in borrowed shoes than she'd imagined.

A root caught her right foot and she nearly fell. Ben turned back long enough to pull her up from a crouch and tug her along, keeping a firm grip on her hand.

"Faster, Anna! They're gaining on us!"

"I...can't...go...any faster!" she huffed.

They reached the car as Frank and Dick Tate burst out of the bushes to their left.

"Hey, you! I know what you..." Frank cried, and then tripped and fell flat on his face.

Dick Tate dropped into a crouch and raised one arm. "Stop or I'll shoot!"

But Anna had already flung herself into the passenger side while Ben hit the starter button. They careened out of the Tate Farm gateway just as a bullet pinged off the back fender.

"Jeepers Creepers, he's really taking pot shots at us!"

Ben floored the accelerator and the tired old car responded like a racehorse.

Anna, huddled into a heap on the passenger side, discovered she was holding her breath.

She twisted around and saw the dark silhouettes of two men, one with gun raised, the other on hands and knees, swaying. No one was following them.

But had they been recognized? Had one of the men taken down Ben's license plate number? She shivered and pulled her coat tighter around herself.

"Are you okay?" asked Ben as he turned onto the main road and headed toward Big Grove.

"Yes. What did you find inside the back of the barn?" asked Anna when she could speak without a betraying tremble.

Ben flashed a grin at her. "Stacks of crates with no labels and a stash of empty whiskey bottles. An old file cabinet I was about to raid when you called me away."

Anna watched his profile. "I didn't think about getting shot at," she said.

"Nor did I," Ben said. "I've never seen either Frank or Dick with a gun. I think I owe you an apology, Anna. I didn't mean to drag you into danger. "

Anna rallied. "I insisted on coming, so it was my choice. My choice and my risk. Though I'm pretty sure my Papa wouldn't see it that way. I'm not planning on telling him about our little adventure, either—at least not right away."

"Attagirl!" said Ben. That heart-stopping grin again. "I knew you were a girl in a million."

Chapter Ten
Early morning in December

A few days later, in a rare moment of quiet companionship, Doc Junker and Martha sipped second cups of coffee at the kitchen table. The twins had just left for school. Franz was still pale and skinny as a stick, but he had recovered most of his energy.

Junker was just thinking how peaceful it was, with the cat Huber sunning himself on the windowsill and the radio burbling, when the telephone shrilled.

"Doc Junker?

"Speaking."

"It's Maisie Busey here, Doc. Marcus is really sick today, and I'm so worried. I can't make him comfortable."

"Does he have a fever?"

"About one hundred degrees. It's the cough—he is so congested, he can hardly take anything."

"Keep the room humidified, and push the fluids on Marcus as much as you can. I will make your house my first stop," Junker promised. He'd been watching young Marcus for several days since he had a cold that had gone to his chest. Pneumonia was looming—a likelihood he hoped to avoid since it was so hard to treat. He drained his coffee and slid his watch chain back into its pocket.

"Going to start your rounds?" Martha asked. "I suppose you know your daughter got in after two a.m. last night." She bustled around the black-and-white kitchen, putting away the leftover coffee cake (cinnamon crumble) and fruit. Next she assembled the ingredients for homemade sausage: local ground pork, fresh garlic, rosemary, and onion. Junker fervently hoped it was on the lunch menu.

"Well, don't be too hard on Anna, *Lieblinge*. She's been a great help with Franz and Emma. And she's doing well in her studies, we can't begrudge her a little fun..."

"Fun!" snorted his wife as she chopped onion. "'Fun' does not two in the morning require! When I was her age, I already work nine months as a nurse..."

Best not to let her continue. "I will be back for lunch, I think," Doc Junker said, collecting his warmest coat and black bag from the closet.

"And how many times have I heard that? In case it is true this time, lunch will be your favorite: garlic-rosemary sausage and mashed potatoes, with apple pie to follow." She gave him a smile, which he returned.

Aha. Sausage for lunch! "Franz will inhale your pie, especially if you pour cream over it. I will make a special effort to be home in good time." He grabbed his fedora and muffler off the hook near the back door.

The weather had cleared, leaving the brick street slick with frost but the air crisp and cold. The Buseys lived in Mahomet, on the edge of the territory Doc Junker covered on rounds. It took him forty-five minutes to get to their farm in the best conditions—more when it rained because the unpaved country roads turned into seas of mud. The front yard had hardly any room for vehicles; it was choked with an old plough, a rusty disc harrow, and a derelict tractor as well as other rubbish.

When Junker knocked on the door, it opened immediately. "Doc Junker!" Mrs. Busey, a slight woman in her thirties, showed signs of incipient hysteria. She snatched his hand and towed him into the bedroom. It stank of menthol and beef broth and musty sheets. A small kettle and towel stood on an end table, no doubt employed to humidify the room as he had instructed.

His patient lay on a narrow bed piled high with quilts underneath a closed window. Marcus was a skinny twelve-year old, dark-haired, with mischievous brown eyes when he wasn't sick. Today, he exhibited clammy, milk-pale skin and a hoarse, productive cough.

"Master Busey," Junker began. "How did you sleep last night?"

"Not so good," croaked Marcus. He tried to sit up but was overtaken with a fit of coughing.

"Is he coughing up anything?" he asked Maisie.

"Yellowish stuff."

Doc Junker picked up the basin off the floor turned Marcus over his arm so the head hung down and tapped the back until the boy coughed up some more into the basin. Hmm. The mucus was thick and pale green. Not good. Junker laid him back on the bed and asked his mother for a full description of recent symptoms.

"He had a bad night," she said, clutching her skirt spasmodically with bony fingers. "Coughing, refusing to drink anything, listlessness…"

Junker offered Marcus a sip of water and then, peered into his nose, and took his temperature. Slightly over one hundred, hmm. Still a low fever, but nothing that could not be controlled with aspirin.

The patient's face looked slightly sunken, as if the flesh had diminished. Gently, Junker pinched the skin on his arm and noted that it did not spring back as well-hydrated skin should. Alarm trickled down his spine. He pulled out his stethoscope and listened to the chest. He heard the telltale bubbling of fluid in the lungs. Pneumonia, then. Damn and double damn!

Doc Junker sat back on the chair and frowned. "Maisie, I want you to give him a cup of broth or water, whatever he'll take, every hour. He's dehydrated in addition to being skinny as a rail."

"But he won't keep anything down!"

"All the more reason to replace fluids, even one sip at a time. And keep humidifying the room with hot water, and put the VapoRub on his chest. I will check back late this afternoon. If he is not improved, I'll admit him to the hospital overnight for intravenous fluids and observation. You have enough cough mixture and aspirin?"

"Yes."

Junker said his goodbyes and trudged back to the car, fighting his unease about this case. Pneumonia was scary in the best of circumstances; beyond humidification, menthol treatment, pushing liquids, and cooling the fever, there wasn't much he could do. The prognosis was worse when a patient was a frail as Marcus. No reserves of strength.

The morning progressed with visits to two pregnant mothers (one very near her time, with a worrisome breach position), one case of Jake Foot, and checking on a boil he'd lanced two days before.

The thought of Martha's sausage and apple pie quickened his steps as Junker strode back to the Tin Lizzie. She chugged her way home, bumping over icy ruts and skidding badly at the intersection of Route 23 and Prospect Ave. Despite the poor road conditions, he enjoyed the ride: the fields were frosted and gleaming under watery sunshine and the cold December air invigorated him.

By the time he'd mounted the steps and opened the back door, Junker was ravenous. Shouts of laughter from his two youngest children greeted him.

"What's the joke?" Junker asked as he unwound his gray-and-red striped muffler. He hung it and his wool fedora on their hook.

"Franz got told off in school today!" Emma announced gleefully.

"Did not!" said Franz with an injured expression.

"Yes, you did! You didn't do your frog report!" Emma bounced away from her brother as he tried to grab her sleeve.

"Did so! I just forgot to bring it..." Franz glanced up at Junker, brown eyes shining with sincerity.

"And probably you did not put it in your satchel last night, am I right?" Junker said.

"Father, I was talkin' with Grandpa and I forgot."

"Naturally," Junker said, rumpling his curls. Thank goodness Franz's behavior had returned to that of a normal, lively seven-year-old.

Grandpa shuffled into the kitchen and made a beeline for his favorite chair.

"Lunch is ready," Martha said.

They drew up their chairs to the new kitchen table. His father sat nearest to the radiator to warm his rheumatic joints and the children sat as far away from each other as possible: one at each corner of the table. Martha sat at one end, Doc Junker at the other. He noticed that Martha looked especially toothsome today, in a housedress that showed more skin than usual...

He really shouldn't be thinking about sex at lunchtime. But then again, why not? A man can dream—and most men he knew fantasized several times a day. Maybe later, she would be in the mood. "Hans is not joining us?" he asked.

"He has band practice over the lunch hour. I sent cold beef and oatmeal-raisin cookies with him this morning," Martha replied.

"Did you save some cookies for me?" demanded Emma.

"Yes, *Liebling*," his wife said.

"Where is my Anna?" Grandpa asked.

"Off to nursing school, after a very late night out," Martha said. "That girl is both ends of the candle burning."

"Applesauce! Why shouldn't she, she is young! It is the time for adventures, for falling in love. And Ben Keck is a reliable fella," Grandpa said, surprising both Doc Junker and his wife. Thomas Earl Junker, Sr. noticed far more than he usually let on, especially about Anna, his favorite grandchild.

"Don't look at me as if I'm half-witted," Grandpa said. "I have all my marbles still, and I can see Anna and Ben fancy each other."

"But I don't want her to become attached the boy next-door!" Martha wailed. "She is beautiful, our Anna! She could have anyone, a doctor, a lawyer..."

"Jumping Jehoshaphat! What does it matter if he is a furniture salesman like his father before him? Ben Keck is made of solid stuff," Grandpa said. "And our Anna is a modern girl. She will be fine, and she will make up her own mind."

"Thomas Earl Junker, I cannot believe what I hear! You know Anna would be better off if we, her parents, choose her husband for her. She has no experience..." Martha was off.

Doc Junker smothered a grin. Usually his father was the traditionalist and Martha argued how modern times meant good changes, like women having the vote and immigrants and Negroes having more opportunities than her parents did. Such discussions often ignored the recent rallies of the Ku Klux Klan practically in their backyard and the lingering hostility towards Germans—and other immigrants—that permeated large parts of their society.

Time to change the subject. "Martha, how about some of that swell apple pie?" Junker said.

Martha cleared the plates and brought the still steaming pie, along with cheddar cheese, thick cream, and fresh coffee, to the table.

Junker sighed with pleasure. Apple pie, the way only Martha could make it.

A difficult birth delayed him in the afternoon, so it was pushing five and the sun was setting in a crimson sky when Doc Junker headed back to the Busey farm.

Mr. Busey, a short scruffy man with a long mustache, met him at the door. "You're too late, Doc Junker," he growled. "My son passed away about half an hour ago. I have no more sons, only a nephew in town." His fists were clenched as if he wanted to punch someone. Probably the doctor in front of him.

"I am so sorry," Junker said, cursing inside. How he hated losing a patient. "May I see him?"

The father stood aside as Junker trod heavily into the bedroom. Maisie wept noisily, bent almost double in the bedside chair. He put a hand on her shoulder. "Maisie? I am so terribly sorry. Tell me what happened."

She turned her pale, tear-drenched face up. "Oh, Doctor, it seemed so sudden. I mean, he slept after you left, but I couldn't wake him for his noon dose of broth...and then his breath got real raspy and he never opened his eyes again."

Doc Junker examined the boy, who lay on his right side. His mouth was slightly open, as if he'd been gasping for air at the end.

Then Junker saw the bottle on the bedside table. Tarnation, dang, and double damn! Blue glass, with a bulbous shape and the now familiar Blue Fire label: "Cough Balm." Not something he had prescribed. Junker snatched it up. "What's this? Maisie, how much of this stuff have you been giving him?"

"Only a few spoonfuls, Doctor, when your medicine didn't work no more..."

"Where did you get it?"

"From that peddler, the one who came around last week." Sadie, the oldest Busey girl, stood in the bedroom doorway.

Junker groaned dismally. Another quack remedy. The fine print on the Cough Balm label read, "Guaranteed to Soothe Throat and Loosen Phlegm and Cure the Common Cold," followed by a long list of other conditions the stuff was supposed to cure. Naturally, the list of ingredients was imprecise: "alcohol, sugars, herbs, flavorings..."

Doc Junker removed the cap and smelled burnt sugar and alcohol. Probably more than thirty-percent alcohol—after all this was a Prohibition product—combined with opiates and goodness knew what else.

Opiates suppressed all the body systems, making it harder for poor Marcus to clear the increasing phlegm from his airways. He couldn't prove it until he had the contents of the bottle tested, but he strongly suspected that Maisie had overdosed her own son with a deadly combination of drugs, herbs, and flavorings that passed for medicine.

He screwed the cap back on the bottle, choosing his words carefully. He commiserated with the family and told them they'd done everything they could for Marcus. And that pneumonia was difficult to treat and that many patients died of it every year despite careful doctoring. Finally, Junker told Maisie to stop buying from peddlers and that she should never mix prescription medicines with home remedies.

She didn't really comprehend what he was trying to tell her—that her over-zealousness had probably killed her son. It was not the right time to press the issue. Junker said his farewells and took the Blue Fire bottle away with him.

Chapter Eleven
The same day, evening

By now it was after six and Doc Junker had a devil of a headache. He wrapped up his throat and hands in his woolies, pulled on his boots, and dragged himself out to the car. Frost shone on the running board, and the cold air snapped under a crescent moon.

He drove home, berating himself for not guessing sooner that Marcus was receiving extra "medicine" that would compound his problems. He felt especially stupid after going through the same experience with his own son!

Even as he cursed his own lack of awareness, he had to admit that accidental overdosing was a common problem throughout his practice and that of every doctor he knew. All his patients had easy access to a huge variety of tonics, balms, liniments, and other elixirs still available through door-to-door peddlers. In his father's day, typical products such as *Hostetter's Stomach Bitters* (with a picture of St. George slaying the dragon of disease on the label) were heavily advertised. Now, people were gulled into buying concoctions such as *Sarsaparilla*, for "Blood Cleansing, Cancers, Tumors, Eruptions, Boils, Scald Head, Ulcers, Lumbago, and Venereal Disease," *Swamp Chill and Fever Tonic*, or *Herbine* to treat "Biliousness, Costiveness, Indigestion, Bloated Abdomen, Wind in the Bowels, and Foul Breath."

Foul Breath, what piffle! He and his fellow physicians were just beginning to understand the complex interactions between prescription medicines and their effects on the human body.

When home remedies with unknown and unregulated proportions of other drugs were added to the mix, the results— and the implications—were terrifying. A doctor could treat a patient using the best, most current medicine and implement a treatment plan knowing full well it could all be undermined by well-meaning but ignorant relatives pushing rubbish on their nearest and dearest.

By the time Junker parked the Tin Lizzie in their garage, his headache had reached the acute pounding stage and all he wanted was a stiff drink and some of Martha's sterling cooking. The telephone rang just as he was hanging up his overcoat and stepping out of his boots.

"Dr. Junker here."

"Doc? It's Jack Searles at the University. I've got bad news for you."

"Tell me."

"I finished the chemical analysis of the bottle that was in Harry Stipes' pocket. There's digitalis in the residue—a hefty dose."

"Damn!" Junker said, unwinding his scarf. "Anything else?"

"Funny you should ask," said Jack. "This Blue Fire bottle matches the size and shape of another one I tested recently, with a label that reads 'Blue Fire Health Tonic, Best Remedy for Man or Beast.' The stuff has lead and cocaine in it as well as digitalis. The combination could fell a horse."

"How much digitalis?" asked Junker uneasily.

"At least double the normal dose," Jack answered. "Hard to see how anyone could be so careless in making it up. What do you want me to do with this information?"

"Nothing right now. Save the bottle, and I'll pick it up tomorrow. I'm in the process of collecting evidence, and when I know more, I'll contact the police."

"Okay, Doc. I trust you to do what's right." Jack's solid analytical chemistry training and his well-equipped laboratory had helped Junker out several times when he needed to know exactly what his patients were imbibing or inhaling.

Doc Junker replaced the receiver on its hook. His first reaction was sheer frustration. Why had Harold Stipes thought he needed a home remedy on top of his prescription medicine, the one Junker had given him? By double-dosing with Blue Fire Heart tonic, he'd essentially committed suicide. He'd imbibed too much digitalis.

His second reaction was fury. If it were suicide, then it was assisted suicide. Someone planned it that way. No way that much digitalis had gotten there accidentally. Harold Stipes had been deliberately poisoned, and Junker thought he knew why. Before Harry felt really ill, he'd been hinting that he was working on a controversial story. Harry liked scandal, but he also followed black market activities and politics. And he liked meaty subjects, larger-than-local issues of the day. He'd done major stories on the Ku Klux Klan in Illinois and clashes between longtime citizens and newly-arrived immigrants. Junker knew Stipes was interested in the bootlegging industry. The two of them had discussed it, ironically while consuming bootleg whiskey. What if Stipes' current story was an exposé on local bootlegging or one of its spinoff industries, such as selling home remedies with high alcohol content? And if so, how could Junker prove it?

It was almost eight o'clock. "Martha, I'm home!" he bawled, hearing voices and laughter upstairs.

"I'm putting the twins to bed," she called. "Your dinner is in the oven."

"Daddy! Don't forget my goodnight kiss!" cried Emma.

"Me too!" Franz yelled.

"I'll be up soon, I promise."

Junker filled a tall glass of water and took his plate of warm meatloaf, mashed potatoes, and green beans with *Spaetzle* out of the oven and sat down at the kitchen table. The food was delicious, as always, but he was too preoccupied to really enjoy it.

Labels were supposed to tell physicians what was in any box, bottle, or packet passed off as medicine, but the first attempt to regulate things, the Food and Drug law of 1906, had been totally swamped by the reality of Prohibition. Making the manufacture and sale of liquor illegal pushed those operations underground. New businesses, large and small, sprang up like weeds after a thunderstorm, often with homemade labels for their products. And why would anyone tell the truth about the exact alcohol and opiate content of a product when lying was so much more profitable? Enforcement was thin on the ground because excise agents—and police—were poorly paid, overworked, and easily bribed.

"Daddy!" called an imperious voice from upstairs.

Junker hauled his weary body upright and went up to kiss his children goodnight.

The children slept, the heady smell of molasses cookies fresh from the oven filled the room, and the cuckoo clock ticked companionably on the shelf over the stove. The Junkers sat around the kitchen table enjoying mugs of hot tea.

"What is it, Earl? Something is bothering you." Martha clasped her hands around her mug and waited.

He looked at her dear face framed with wisps of graying blond hair, her skin still rosy from giving the children their baths. Thank goodness, he could talk to his wife. They had their ups and downs, but Martha showed good sense and understanding about everything—except her family's consumption of liquor. She was also discreet; Junker knew anything he told her would be kept close to her ample bosom.

"I've lost another patient today. You know about Harold Stipes, but this afternoon Marcus Busey died." He filled her in.

Martha clapped a hand over her mouth. "Poor little Marcus! I will have to visit Maisie and take her some food. And you think she...her own son overdosed? Just like Franz! Oh, how terrible!"

"Indeed—and worse, she scarcely realizes her error. It makes me so angry. Such deaths could be prevented if people were better informed—and if home remedies were not so commonplace and easy to obtain."

"Education is the answer," Martha said. "Nurses and doctors' assistants could be better informed, and then they train housewives. That can be a beginning."

Junker nodded. Easier said than done. "That, and achieving a higher level of trust between doctors and patients. My father discovered time and again that his rural patients didn't really trust physicians who had any formal training. He said city docs were too fancy to their way of thinking, not to mention too expensive. Today, most of them still believe their grandmas have better remedies than any physician, and so they're all the more credulous when a peddler shows up at the front door."

Martha sighed. "I know better, but I caught Anna just last week, at the front door, looking over a peddler's 'skin enhancements' and cosmetics. I gave the fella a flea in his ear and sent him away. I told him if I saw him on Elm Boulevard again, I would warn all our neighbors to shun him."

"You'd think she'd be less credulous after what happened to her little brother."

"Yes, but she thought cosmetics were different—not medicinal."

"Huh. I suppose I can see her point of view, but it's just one more example of products for sale that we know nothing about." Junker told Martha about the chemist's findings, but implied that the death was due to drug interactions rather than deliberate murder. He didn't want to scare his wife—nor did he want to discuss bootlegging. She would turn their chat into a rant about her father Hans Friedrich's low-down drunken ways.

Martha surprised him by introducing the topic of hooch herself as she refilled their mugs. "Earl, I know you have other things on your mind, but Anna told me Tommy Crouch is drinking too much."

Junker grimaced. "Yes, and in public. Anna and I have both seen him half seas over. I wish I knew what was eating him. I can't afford to have my assistant incapacitated."

"I think I know," said Martha with a sudden smile.

He raised his eyebrows.

"He likes our Anna too much."

"Good Heavens!" Such an idea had never occurred to him before, but now that he thought about it...Tommy tended to avoid his employer's gaze whenever Anna was mentioned. And he was awfully protective of her. Hmm.

"Don't worry," Martha said. "He won't ever tell her—he knows it's impossible with the age difference. And I have a plan."

Martha's plans usually involved either temperance or matchmaking. "Well?"

"I know a nice young widow who's looking for a husband."

"Poor Tommy," Junker said. "He's as good as hitched already."

Martha went to bed early, exhausted after a busy day of meetings and childcare. Doc Junker settled down at the kitchen table with another cup of tea (this time with a tiny addition of whiskey, with butter and honey).

Someone knocked on the back door. Junker peered out at the dark shape on the back porch and flung open the door. "Gerry! Just the person I wanted to see. Come on in."

Gerry accepted a mug of doctored tea and took a chair. "I was visiting Hank two streets over and thought I'd stop by. How's business?"

Junker said he'd just lost another patient.

"That's hard. I'm sorry, Illinois, I know how hard it is to try to help people."

"And I think bootlegging around here is getting out of hand."

"Bootlegging, making moonshine, or both? I know we've talked about how folks use grain alcohol and car radiators to make home brews and rot their insides. So what is it now?"

"Many of my patients are exacerbating their medical problems by drinking hooch—both the stuff that gets shipped in from out-of-state and locally manufactured tarantula juice."

Gerry swallowed some of his hot brew. "It doesn't help that the excise agents are incapable of enforcing anything."

Doc Junker tipped back his chair (a habit he knew Martha hated—that's probably why he kept doing it). "You are so right. I've seen agents being given free drinks and discreet wads of cash."

"So have I. Why, I've seen how the bartender at the Steamroom keeps extra cash and high-grade whiskey on hand just for the agents!"

"I expect so. But there's more, Gerry. The same fellas who

are making or transporting whiskey are also producing home remedies that are just as bad as moonshine made in lead-lined radiators." Junker told him the sorry tale of Marcus Busey and the results of the chemical tests on Stipes' bottle. "...and it came up as toxic soup, with extra digitalis and other compounds that oughta be better controlled. Silly fool thought he needed something besides what I gave him. He overdosed just like Marcus, from a combination of his prescription medicine from me and the alcoholic home remedy he bought somewhere locally. Difference between the two cases is that someone *wanted* Stipes dead and added the extra digitalis."

"Good God! And this on top of what happened to your Franz! But I don't understand," said Gerald. "Why are you so sure the digitalis was added by someone besides the manufacturer?"

"It's like this: I think Harold Stipes may have been chasing after a local bootleg operation..." Junker explained about Harry's hints and his previous history of choosing controversial topics for his reporting.

"So now you have two problems: drug interaction between bad booze, prescription medicines and home remedies, and deliberate murder."

"And I am very much afraid the two deaths may be connected," Junker said grimly. "Both the cough balm and the tonic had the same label: 'Blue Fire.' "

"Wait a minute, why would the Blue Fire people sell both whiskey and home remedies? Isn't whiskey much more profitable?" asked Gerry.

"Maybe, if you cut the good stuff with one of those molasses, yeast, and water concoctions and rebottle it. But the tonics are everywhere—people buy them. Especially rural folk. Sometimes I think I see more home remedies in my practice than my father did twenty years ago."

Gerry took another solid swig of tea and whiskey and scratched his head. "I guess I'm surprised ordinary folks don't make their own tonics at home along with their bathtub gin."

"Well, if they realized that most tonics are no more than grain alcohol, water, herbs, and flavorings with no magical ingredients added, I expect they would. Those door-to-door peddlers are great advertisers. You know the kind of stuff: 'this here tonic will cure everything from rheumatism to indigestion, impotency, and hair loss.'"

Gerry grinned. "So what you're saying is that the Blue Fire guys are pushing both hooch and home remedies that contribute directly or indirectly to patient deaths. If that's true, there are probably all kinds of people out there getting really ill—or dying—the same way! What are you going to do, Illinois?"

"Collect more evidence, first of all. You can help me, Gerry, by keeping an eye out for any bottle labeled 'Blue Fire.' I'd really like to prevent more patients from killing themselves if I can. And find out who thought Harold Stipes was such a threat that he had to be poisoned.

"Big Grove is getting unhealthy. First Harold, then Franz, now Marcus. Who's next?"

Chapter Twelve
Saturday afternoon

Anna adjusted the strap on her left Mary Jane shoe, fretting that Ben was late.

He'd been at work until four-thirty and she'd been at the medical library. He was supposed to meet her at Vriner's at four forty-five, and he said he had a surprise for her. Anna was panting to know what it was—she had a feeling Ben had been up to something since their midnight trek.

It was now well after five o'clock and the younger party crowd was filling up the speakeasies as families left the ice cream joints for home and supper. Anna found herself at a dark booth near the back of the store, near the candy-cane making apparatus. She was starving. Should she order a sandwich, or maybe a chocolate soda?

Ben whooshed through the front door, scanning the booths for Anna. Her heart suddenly buoyant, she waved at him. He shoved his golfer onto the back of his head and undid his raccoon coat as he strode toward her. Anna noticed that several other feminine gazes followed him as he slid onto the bench across from her.

"You're a sight for sore eyes, Anna. Is that a new hat?"

"Yes." Her cheeks grew warm. What a good thing she'd picked up the dark green hat with upturned brim on sale. She knew the sweeping feathers went well with her blond hair and made her eyes look a darker blue. Never mind that her pocket money had evaporated; it was worth it if Ben Keck noticed.

He spied her looking at the blackboard. "Let me guess—

91

you're starving."

"Yes."

Ben laughed and motioned to the waiter. "What will you have?"

"Cheese sandwich and a chocolate soda."

"Make that two chocolate sodas, and give me a ham-and-swiss on rye, no mustard," Ben said. He pulled his coat off, extracted a sheaf of papers from the inside pocket, and flung the discarded coat on the bench next to him. "Here's my little surprise. I went back to Tate Farm this morning, early, when no one was around. I got into that file cabinet."

"Ben! You took quite a chance going back there! Though I can't say, this time that I wish you'd taken me with you."

Ben laughed. "I haven't had time to look at these, so let's do it together," he said, spreading the papers out so they could both examine them.

Anna glowed, pleased that he'd waited to share the discovery with her. She bent her head over the documents. "Invoices," she said after a moment. "But what peculiar names!"

"Health Elixir, Sarsaparilla Extract, Blue Fire Purgative, Amargo Aromatico—look, this one's for 'internal stomach disorders.' Whew." Ben read the names aloud. "High prices, too. Look, this Elixir sells for $3.15 a bottle."

"Here's my favorite," said Anna. "'Blue Fire Liniment for Man or Beast. Cure for What Ails You.'"

Ben snorted. "Sure. Probably three parts panther piss whiskey and a few herbs for window dressing. Here's another one, a cough balm that 'soothes the windpipe and cures the common cold.'"

Anna gasped. "Oh my gosh, here's a Heart Tonic! This is probably the stuff Harold Stipes was carrying!"

"Does your Dad have proof it had anything to do with his death?"

"All I know is, he sent the stuff off to be tested at the University."

"Any results yet?"

"He hasn't said anything."

Ben scanned the list again. "I bet your father is familiar with all of these. He must encounter all kinds of stuff in his practice."

"Not just familiar," Anna said, looking straight into Ben's luminous eyes. "He's kind of on a crusade right now, trying to get people to stop using these un-prescribed 'cures' in place of- or on top of—real medicine. Says it complicates being a doctor, and sometimes kills people. But he also told me the big money isn't in home remedies, it's whiskey—and gin and rum."

Ben smiled grimly and pointed to an entry farther down the invoice sheet. "'Buttermilk.' Ha. How much do you want to bet that is whiskey or another liquor that has nothing to do with dairy products? My Dad says he read about a truck being stopped by the feds. It had a load of 'buttermilk' bottles, but when they were opened, the contents proved to be high-grade Georgia corn whiskey. Another case, the stuff in the truck bed was legit, but there was a false bottom with flasks of giggle water piled underneath."

"I know a lot of girls who carry hooch in their boot flasks or strapped around their waist under coats."

"And I know a lot of fellas who carry the stuff in spare tires and under the hoods of their cars so they can offer drinks to their girls wherever they go," said Ben. "Anyhow, I'm guessing this Blue Fire outfit is making someone a lot of jack."

"But who's running it?" Anna asked.

"Who do you think? My money's on Big Bruce Donaldson. He has the speakeasy and the local connections."

"Do we go to the police?"

"Nah. At least, not yet. Two of our local cops take bribes from both the excise agents and blind pig owners."

"How do you know all this?" asked Anna.

Ben smiled sheepishly. "Frank—and others—have told me."

"We need to tell my father everything we've found out," Anna said with a frown. "But he'll be out on his rounds until eight or nine tonight because he has hospital hours as well today."

"The sooner the better," agreed Ben. "This stuff is dynamite, and it's bigger than we can manage on our own."

Chapter Thirteen
Late that night

Junker poured a small whiskey and padded to his favorite chair next to the radio. After another hard day traipsing around the county and a late arrival home, he found himself the last one awake in the house at ten pm. He was grateful to be warm and dry, knowing full well that it was sleeting and miserable outside. The tick-tock of the kitchen clock harmonized with his father's sonorous snoring next door. Junker, Sr., kept to his lifelong habit of early to bed and even earlier rising—usually before Martha started the bacon and coffee.

He opened his book (the latest Sinclair Lewis) and was soon lost in the banal life of George Babbitt. He'd lost track of time a sharp report from next door jerked him out of the story.

Boom!

Two gun shots! If the first shot was a pistol, the second one sure sounded like a shotgun.

Junker flung down his book and hurried to the back door. He undid the bolt as quietly as he could and stepped out onto the ice-covered porch. Nothing was stirring at the Keck's house next door, but that's where the sounds had come from. Unless he was hearing an echo off another building...

Suddenly the Keck's back door banged as a slim figure in a long coat and brimmed hat rushed out, catapulted off the back steps, and hightailed it for the alley.

"Hey!" Junker yelled. Then, as the figure turned and fired a wild shot at him, he ducked. The man sped away to the west behind the Harris house.

Ben Keck appeared in the doorway and spotted him. "Doc Junker! We need your help! My father's been shot."

"Be right there," Junker said. He ducked back inside, grabbed his black bag and a hat against the sleet, and slithered across the yard in his slippers. Ben and his mother met him at their back door. Linda Keck carried her husband's shotgun. The reek of black powder filled the air—smelled like she'd just fired it.

"Thank goodness you're here, Illinois." Linda's short gray hair stood up in spikes around her head but her eyes were steady. "Mathew's been shot in the arm. The miserable scallywag who did it escaped through the front door before I could do more than make him dance."

Junker was surprised she hadn't killed him while she had the chance. "What happened? Was it a burglary?" he asked.

"Probably. I was asleep when the shooting started..." Linda began.

"Yes, but they didn't get what they were looking for," said Ben.

Junker glanced at him sharply. "They? How many of them were there?"

"Two," he replied. "The slim guy in the fedora who fired at you and a second, chunkier fella who scarpered through the front door."

"Come along, Illinois. Matt's in the front room. I think the bullet went clean through the flesh." Linda still carried the shotgun.

By now they were in the parlor, identical in size and shape to Doc Junker's surgery. Matthew Keck sat in a wing chair, clutching his left arm below the elbow. Blood stained his shirt and had spotted the upholstery. His face was beaded with sweat and his eyes dilated with shock.

"Let me clean that off and have a look," Junker said, opening his bag. "If Linda is right about the bullet, I may not have to take you next door to my surgery. No need, if there's no bullet to remove."

"Kinda handy to have a doctor next door for these occasions," Matthew quipped. "Not that we do this very often…Ow!"

"Sorry. Keep supporting that arm with your other hand."
Junker used a small scissors to slit the shirtsleeve up to
Mathew's armpit and pulled away the cloth. Gently, he probed
the area with his fingertips as he looked for an exit wound. It
was there, on the backside of his upper arm. "You're in luck,
Matt. A little alcohol, inside and out, and you'll be as good as
new. Arm will be a bit sore for several days, though. Ben, hand
me that sling from the outside pocket of my bag, would you?"

Ben, who'd been hovering at his shoulder, deftly dug out
what Junker needed and passed it to him, along with the second
roll of gauze. Suddenly Junker noticed his daughter, Anna,
standing just behind Ben. "What in tarnation are you doing
here?" Junker groused. "You might have been shot crossing the
yard."

"So might you," she retorted. Her blond curls set off her
wide blue eyes and rumpled purple flannel nightgown. "I heard
the shots, Father, and I knew Ben had just got home…"

Now they were getting somewhere—she'd been out with
young Ben again. "Wait," he said. "Has anyone telephoned the
police?"

"Ben wouldn't let me for some reason," complained Linda,
who had just given her husband a hefty tot of brandy.

Junker pinned his gaze on Ben's suddenly grim face. "Why
on earth wouldn't you call the police? And what did you mean
by saying earlier that they hadn't gotten what they came for?"

Ben said, "We were going to tell you…" he paused and
looked at Anna.

"Papa, it's like this. We followed Frank Donaldson a few
nights ago…"

Now that they'd started on their story, they couldn't get it
out fast enough. After several interruptions, Junker finally
understood that a) they'd been at the Tate Farm, b) Ben had
stolen some invoices, and c) his darling daughter had been
zipping around the county in the middle of the night with a
young man he could stand to know better, much better. Martha
didn't need to know about this escapade…yet.

"Let's see the invoices," he said as soon as Anna had paused for breath.

Ben cleared a space on a side table and Linda pressed a glass of brandy into Junker's willing hands before she left the room to tuck her husband into bed.

"See, Father, here's the heart tonic invoice."

Junker skimmed the paper. "Very interesting—quite a haul you two got." He glanced through the other invoices. Blue Fire was obviously doing a thriving business in liquor and home remedies. "So who's running it?" he said out loud.

Ben said, "Sir, I think the outfit has to have a local connection since Frank and Bruce Donaldson seem to know about it. And their stash is not so far from downtown Big Grove."

"Did you see Big Bruce out there?"

"No, but when we saw Big Bruce at the Steamroom, I had the impression he'd passed something to Frank."

"You didn't tell me that!" interrupted Anna.

"I thought you'd seen it too." Ben turned back to him. "And Big Bruce is Frank's boss." He stared at the floor. "I wasn't going to say anything about how odd Frank has been lately, but Frank is my buddy and I'm worried. I think he's gotten himself in over his head and he needs some kind of help. The fellas he mixes with are no darn good."

Junker's respect for the young man soared. Ben was impetuous, but he had a good enough character to express concern for a friend and be willing to stick his neck out. He could tell from his daughter's rapt gaze on Ben's face that she thought he was pretty swell, too.

As he ruminated over his next move, he suddenly noticed the Big Grove Gazette on the low table in front of the fire. "Jeepers Creepers! Hand me that front page, will you, Anna?"

Mystified, she passed it over.

The photograph on page one was familiar. In fact, it was identical to the photograph Harold Stipes had had in his pocket when he died. Junker peered at the caption: "Bernie Shelton, member of southern Illinois bootlegging gang."

He showed it to Anna and Ben. "Ben, this outfit is bigger than local. I think my friend Stipes was working on an article about statewide bootlegging…"

Ben interrupted. "But we can't go to the police yet.

Junker thought about that. He didn't trust Han the Hun (a.k.a. Captain Stoltman); in fact he could only think of one local cop who didn't take bribes. "I agree. I'd like a little more proof before I bring anyone else into this. You may be right that Bruce Donaldson is the big cheese. But if he is…" He glared at the two youngsters. "Then he's dangerous. And you two stay out of it."

"But Papa!"

"But Doc Junker! I want to help. I agree that Anna should be kept out of it…" Ben winced as Anna gave him a withering look. "Maybe you can think of something we can do that's not dangerous."

"Hmph. I'll need to sleep on that," Junker said. "Now off to bed with you both. It's late."

Chapter Fourteen
Sunday morning

Doc Junker slept poorly as Saturday night faded into Sunday. Martha snored peacefully beside him while he fought with his pillow and wrestled over what steps to take next. Stipes deserved to be avenged; so did poor Marcus Busey. If Junker played his cards right, he could rumble the entire Blue Fire operation.

But he had to move carefully. The network of blind pig owners all looked after each other. They, and the police and excise agents who accepted bribes, wouldn't take kindly to any action that would curtail their income. And reputations, maybe lives, were at stake: no one wanted to be known as a snitch.

The only ally Junker could think of was young Graziano Fellini, a skinny young cop who already had the reputation for unusual service above and beyond what his department expected. He liked to work undercover, dressed as a seedy bar hopper in an old suit and a disreputable fedora. Out of uniform, he changed his normal stride to a shuffle and held one shoulder higher than the other so he looked crooked. Junker had seen Fellini completely fool folks who thought they knew him.

He punched the pillow again and rolled over to face the window. The main problem was proof. Junker had to ascertain first, that Bruce Donaldson really was the big cheese, second, determine the scope of his operation, and third, choose the best time to turn him in. There was so much Junker didn't know: who were Big Bruce's contacts inside Big Grove? Did he have a direct link to the Shelton gang in Little Egypt, as the photo in

Stipes' pocket suggested? Was the Blue Fire distribution confined to Big Grove (that he doubted) and if not, how far did it extend?

Unable to sleep, Doc Junker got up and padded down to the kitchen for a glass of warm milk and to make a list. He sat at the table and forced his muddled mind to concentrate enough to write. One: focus on the local connections first—enlist Fellini's help. Two: keep Anna and Ben busy by giving them a job, but what? He stared at the relentlessly ticking cuckoo clock. Maybe they could look specifically for Blue Fire products and connections to Bruce Donaldson while visiting the speakeasies. Junker knew that he couldn't stop them from going out, but he wanted to scare them a little.

Query: he'd heard Bruce owned several businesses downtown. How many speakeasies did he run, and where were they? Besides, he needed to update Fellini on the chemist's findings about Stipes' death; Fellini had heard about the death from his boss, Captain Stoltman, but at that time the evidence pointed to natural causes. And maybe Fellini could detail someone to keep an eye on Anna and Ben. They mustn't forget that Stipes was poisoned, probably deliberately, and that there was now a definite link between his death and regional bootlegging.

And—brilliant thought—Junker could kill two birds with one stone by taking Tommy along to some of the speakeasies and find out what was bugging him. They'd form two teams, Anna and Ben, and Tommy and himself. Another thing he didn't plan to tell Martha about until it was all over.

The warm milk, combined with a coherent action plan, made him sleepy. He went back to bed as dawn sent slender fingers of light through the bedroom curtain.

Later that afternoon, he met with Anna and Ben in the Keck's kitchen.

Junker explained his plan. Anna and Ben listened, but they exchanged several glances and smiles and seemed overly pleased with themselves.

Junker paused. "I hope you two aren't treating this as a

game. What I'm asking you to do is serious research."

"Yeah, but it sure beats work," said Ben.

"And it certainly is unusual," added Anna. "Not the sort of thing a father usually asks his daughter to do! I suppose we're not mentioning this to Mama?"

Doc Junker rubbed his beard. "What do you think? Grandpa would understand, but she'll just think we're all drinking too much. Look, there's something I haven't told you yet." He explained about the chemistry report and the amount of extra digitalis in the Blue Fire bottle Stipes carried.

Anna's face went white. "Then he was poisoned! Grandpa guessed it right! How awful."

Ben took her hand.

"So we are all going to treat this investigation as potentially dangerous." Junker sighed. "You've got to understand, bootleggers usually have guns..."

He stopped, staring at his daughter's transparent expression of guilty alarm.

There was a ghastly pause. Junker waited while Anna tried to school her face back into something approaching calm and Ben, who had a much better poker face, looked straight ahead. "Hmm. There's something you left out of your story from the other night, I think. Somebody shoot at you?"

Anna gasped.

Ben said simply, "Yes, sir. But we got away." He told Doc Junker about their visit to Tate Farm.

Junker glared at the two of them. "So you don't need another lecture from me about being careful. I should lock up the two of you so you can't get into any more trouble..."

"No!" cried Anna and Ben together.

Junker rubbed his hair with both hands. "Martha will kill me when she hears the whole story. She'll say I am a terrible father to you, Anna. I will let you help, but it's only because I know you'll both be in the speakeasies anyway." He thought a moment. "Okay, you've been spotted once. How about you two disguise yourselves before you go to the speaks? It won't fool Frank and Dick, but it might fool other fellas who are assigned to watch for you."

Anna's eyes shone. "I have a red wig!" She turned to Ben. "And I have some costume stuff Hans used last Halloween. There's a moustache that's just the right color for you."

Ben nodded. "I can slick my hair a different direction, too. And wear a different style cap than I usually do."

"Try to keep a low profile, and if anyone bothers you, get out and tell me." Junker said. "By the way, if you are going to visit several joints in one evening, try to alternate the hooch with cranberry juice."

Anna looked superior. "As if I didn't know how to do that already, Papa!"

"Right. We understand each other. Let's make a list of the local speakeasies and blind pigs to visit. We've been to the Steamroom, but someone should go again to watch for the Donaldsons and check for Blue Fire labels. Tommy and I will do that. Now, there's Hell's Half Acre, the Cat's Pajamas, the Silver Slipper, the Blind Lemon..."

"Don't forget the Mazuma Pit, The Rusty Nail, Willy's Whiskers, Cosmopolitan Hall, the Grand Descant, and the Black Meow," said Anna.

"And Dora's Dive, Jake's Joint, Palooka Place, and the Real McCoy." Ben grinned at Junker's expression.

"Naturally, you two have already been to all these places," Junker said dryly.

"Naturally." Anna widened her eyes innocently.

"Hmmph." He'd made two columns on his list. "What about outside of town, but within driving distance? We mustn't forget places in Mahomet and Tolono and St. Joseph."

"Well, there's the Nine Gal Tavern, that Vinegar Hill joint in Danville, the No Name Saloon, Kelly's Roadhouse, Castle Farm..."

"For crying out loud! How many of *those* juice joints have you visited, Ben?"

He smiled sheepishly. "All of them. But, you know what, I bet there are quite a few others we haven't even heard of, and I know how to find out."

"How?" asked Anna.

"Frank Donaldson, of course."

Junker eyed him with respect. "You will, of course, disguise your interest."

"Of course! I'll just say my sheba and I want a little variety, some new gin mills, some new drinks. He'll give me a list..."

"And very likely some of those places will turn out to have a connection with Bruce Donaldson."

"Best of all, Frank won't suspect a thing. He's always boasting about how many out-of-the-way juice joints he frequents—prides himself on knowing more than the rest of us—and he will have the added satisfaction of sending business his uncle's way."

"Okay, we have quite a list here. You two go at it, and we'll meet in say, a week's time and compare notes. Agreed?"

"Pos-i-tive-ly," said Anna.

Chapter Fifteen
Monday morning

Monday rounds included a visit to Nathan Donaldson, ostensibly to check on his progress with the bum leg and the Thomas splint. Doc Junker figured this was the perfect opportunity to quiz Nathan about the peripatetic fence at the Tate Farm.

He found Nathan in a surly mood. Was he in pain, or just hung over? "How's the leg?"

"Not so hot. Thought you said that splint would fix me up so I could get around," growled Nathan.

"What I said was that the splint would help you walk, but that didn't mean you'd be pain-free or that you should overdo traipsing around the countryside. This kind of wound takes more than a couple of weeks to heal completely. Especially since the bullet nicked the bone. Have you been taking the pain medication I gave you?"

"Bah! Whiskey works better."

"I dare say. But it's not as good for your liver." Doc Junker examined the leg and pronounced it as coming along nicely. "You won't need the Thomas splint much longer. Maybe another ten days. By the way Nate, I don't appreciate getting shot at just because I'm near one of your diggings."

Nathan's skimpy eyebrows contracted. "What the hell are you talking about?"

"Oh, don't pretend innocence, you old bugger! Last month, when I was checking on young Tate's arm and stumbled upon the site near the Salt Fork. You and your son took a potshot at me."

Nathan snorted. "It wasn't me. I was on the road to Farmer City with a horse trailer."

"Really?" Nathan wasn't a liar, exactly, but he liked to embroider the truth—or leave crucial information out of his statements. "If it wasn't you or your son, then who was it?"

"Beats me. You know that it's the Wild West out there—everyone trespassing on each other's property lookin' for arrowheads and prettier stuff, like ceramics and skulls and such."

That about summed up Nathan Donaldson's idea of archaeology: take the pretty stuff and toss the rest. Junker decided to abandon the question of who had shot at him for the moment. "Speaking of trespassing, it sure looked to me like someone moved the fence line near your dig. Who's the owner of the adjacent property?"

Nathan's gaze shifted somewhere left of Junker's head. He ruminated a while. Junker wondered if he was going to answer at all when he said, "Well, actually the southern parcel still belongs to the Tates, and the northern parcel belongs to our family. I have digging rights on anything I own, so naturally I wanted the fence to run inside the Donaldson boundary. I figured the Tates would never even notice."

"Naturally." Junker agreed, reflecting that Nathan had always been careless with other people's property when he wanted something. "Nathan, I've seen some of your brother's employees hanging around the old Tate barn. What are they doing out there, if it's not even Donaldson land?"

"How should I know? I'm not my brother's keeper. Maybe they like to fish in the stream, like Bruce. And if you were out there, I bet you were messing with my site!"

"I didn't take anything. And if I had, I'd have done some drawings and taken photos and not just yanked it out of the ground."

"Yeah, you think you're a scientist."

"I care about record-keeping, that's all. History is all about context, not just isolated objects. You can't learn anything about the people who used the objects without knowing something about…"

"Oh, get off your high horse! Don't lecture me about saving everything.

"Fine. Let's go back to your brother. Big Bruce is your son Frank's employer, isn't he?"

"So? Frank needs a firm hand. I'm glad his uncle takes an interest in him."

"What if uncle Bruce is leading your son astray?" asked Junker.

"What the devil do you mean by that?"

Doc Junker eyed Nathan, noting his high color and indignant tone. Hmm. He had the feeling Nathan was trying to pull the wool over his eyes. "I think your brother and your nephew are involved in bootlegging. Here in Champaign County. There's a great deal of booze with funny labels cropping up in funny places."

Nathan seemed to deflate. "Well, my younger brother always was a wild one. He might be leasing Tate Farm's barn as a storehouse for something. Might even be liquor, for all I know. He has his fingers in a great many pies. "

"Frank spends much of his time at the speakeasies."

"And your daughter doesn't? Do you know anybody who doesn't frequent the juice joints?"

"I sure do. My wife Martha."

"Ha, ha! The Temperance Queen."

Junker permitted himself a small smile. Nathan wasn't much help, and everything he said was perfectly plausible. He sounded ignorant of his brother's activities but still managed to cast suspicion on Bruce Donaldson.

Time to complete his rounds—and drum up some better sources of information.

Chapter Sixteen
Tuesday evening

Ben and Anna picked their way between broken bricks on Market St. and entered the back entrance of a two-story house with a wrap-around porch that probably dated to the founding of Big Grove. The entryway smelled of cat pee—how appropriate for a blind pig called "The Cat's Pajamas." They climbed a rickety flight of wooden stairs and knocked at the narrow door. The door creaked open and a tall, bearded drink of water said, "Password?"

"The Bees' Knees."

"Enter."

Ben and Anna stepped into a small sitting room that looked like—and probably was—a converted bedroom. It was jammed with clients, perching at tiny round tables or leaning against the wall.

"What's yours?" asked the bartender, the same man who had let them in. He stood in a curious recess in the wall, behind a five-foot-high cabinet that served as a bar.

"A cranberry gin sling for the lady and whiskey and ice for me." Ben figured they'd be more likely to see Blue Fire products if he ordered hard liquor. He shed his camelhair coat—it was his father's—and handed it to Anna. "Get us a table, hon."

Ben fingered his false moustache inhaled the familiar reek of cigarette smoke and cheap gin altered with herbs. He looked around for familiar faces, but saw no one he recognized. A good start to their evening out. It was kind of fun to be incognito in his own hometown.

He watched the bartender, who was almost certainly the owner of the house as well as the blind pig. So far, Ben had visited blind pigs behind a steam laundry, above a lawyer's office, in back of an ice cream parlor, and next to a carriage and tire shop. This was his first venture into a private home. He glanced around for Anna, who'd found a table squished into the corner of the room and winked at her. She looked exotic in her red wig. Anna had borrowed a pink dress with an uneven hem from Sally and punched up her makeup with dark lipstick and eye-shadow. The normally delicate pink of her skin was heightened to a deep rose with sheer excitement. Ben himself felt more than usually keyed up; he wanted to satisfy Doc Junker by completing their mission successfully and he certainly wanted to keep dating Anna.

To Ben's delight, the bartender produced a squat bottle with a familiar blue logo. "Hey, that's a new one—can I see it?"

The man shot him an odd look, but passed the bottle over. "It's high-quality stuff. We only serve the best here. We do set-ups too, if you'd rather drink your own poison."

Ben examined the bottle. This one claimed to be "Blue Fire Corn Whiskey, produced in central Illinois by Blue Fire Distributors." Interesting—so the outfit called itself a "distributor." More likely, the bootleggers purchased medium-grade whiskey from Canada or Missouri and cut it with their own mixture. Ben wondered how far away the bottling facility was—Danville? Peoria?

"Thanks," he said as he paid for the drinks. "I'm sure it's good stuff. I'm a collector of labels—the fancier the better. I haven't seen the Big Blue Stem logo before."

"Well, it stands to reason they'd put prairie grass on liquor from around here," the bartender said. He picked up a grungy cloth and wiped the sticky top of the cabinet.

"Who'd ya buy from?" asked Ben rashly.

The bushy eyebrows of the proprietor descended into a horizontal line. "Now, young fella, don't start asking too many questions. I might begin to think you're an agent—or a reporter."

"Sorry," Ben said. "Didn't mean to be nosy." He beat a retreat to the corner, carrying the two drinks.

"So, what did you find out?" Anna leaned eagerly toward him.

"Easy does it. I think we should wait until we're outside to exchange information. Too crowded in here." He put his hand over hers to make it look like they were just being friendly.

Anna responded by squeezing his hand and giving him an intimate smile. "So, we're just a sheik and his sheba out for a drink, right?"

"That's right." Ben felt a glow somewhere near his solar plexus at Anna's admission of their new relationship. He hadn't been sure until that moment what she thought of their deepening friendship, especially since he'd kissed her only once. That had been a tentative kiss because they'd been in her parent's house; next time he meant to do it better—and longer.

"Sip your drink slowly—it's going to be a long night. We'll move on to the next juice joint in about twenty minutes."

They exchanged inconsequential remarks on the daringly low-cut dress (black, with a fringe) of the woman two tables away, the weather, and Ben's new hairdo (combed flat so it looked longer).

Suddenly a buzzer rang.

All the customers moved quickly. Some chugged their drinks, others nipped up to the bar and gave the bartender their glasses. Ben grabbed Anna's drink and his own and handed them over. The bartender pushed a button on the wall to his right and hidden sliding doors activated. In thirty seconds, bar, bartender, and liquor had all disappeared behind a false wall. A framed landscape painting descended from the ceiling to cover the thin line made by the closed doors.

Ben laughed at the expression of surprise on Anna's face. "It's a raid, hon. Let's follow the others out." He pointed to a second door. This led to stairs descending below the level of the street. Soon they found themselves in a surprisingly clean steam tunnel lit by dim lights. After climbing a narrow second set of stairs, the customers emerged in a hallway that let them out onto Walnut Street. Everyone dispersed quickly.

"Well, that was interesting. I had no idea there was a tunnel here! I guess this means we find another gin mill," Anna said.

"Attagirl! Let's try the Silver Slipper. It's above a shoe store on north First Street. Word is, you can get 'a shoeshine and some moonshine' in the same establishment."

Two hours later, they were awash in drink (liquor alternating with fruit juice or shandies) and Ben was growing tired. Anna, however, looked perky and ready for an all-nighter. Her eyes shone with mischief and her borrowed clothing was unstained and fresh. Ben, on the other hand, felt rumpled and a bit seedy. Perhaps he couldn't hold his liquor as well as he thought.

They clutched cold glasses of near-beer at a little joint called the Blind Lemon, a second-floor walkup on Market Street. It was a private home, with three staircases, and the drinks were served through a tube that led to a third floor bedroom. As Ben had explained to Anna on their way over, the booze was dispensed down the tube by the proprietor's ten-year-old son.

"Frank told me they have a system of knocks: three knocks for whiskey, two for beer, one for gin. The kid upstairs pours a measured amount down the tube and the father dispenses it. If an excise agent shows up on the first floor, mamma presses a buzzer. Papa pushes a button that makes the tube retract into a hole in the ceiling, while upstairs Junior closes the trap door, pulls a throw rug over it, and strews his homework artistically over the rug. Some arrangement, isn't it?"

Anna laughed. "Sure is. I'm sure those parents would get into a heap of trouble if the agents knew how they were employing their son."

"Of course, but the Burwashes are smart. They've been raided before. The family just waits a week or so and starts up again. The feds suspect illegal booze is sold here but they've never caught the family red-handed."

"And I suppose the setup is no more unusual than a whole family making bathtub gin on a Sunday afternoon."

"Well, most folks keep the homemade stuff for private consumption. Like my mom—she makes an herb-infused vodka. But as long as you don't try to sell it, you don't get into trouble." Ben stood up. "I think I'll see what kind of snacks they have. If we're going to a couple more places, I need something besides liquid in my stomach."

He sauntered over to the makeshift bar—this time the top of a player piano. Ben figured the glasses were hidden behind the keyboard lid when the place was raided.

"My date would like some nuts or pretzels if you have them," said Ben.

"Sure thing," Mr. Burwash replied, handing Ben a dish of peanuts. "And a refill for you, young fella?"

"Not just yet," Ben said. "Say, do you carry that Blue Fire stuff? The high-grade whiskey?"

"Yeah, what's it to ya?" Burwash's tone chilled noticeably.

"Just curious. It's nice stuff, and not every speak carries it." Ben had tried variants on his initial query at each joint they visited. The reactions of the proprietors ranged from surprise to downright hostility.

"Well, Blue Fire whiskey is expensive and not for everyone."

A skinny fella in a grubby fedora motioned to Ben from the table closest to the piano. "Hey, young Keck. Come over here."

Ben complied, surprised that the man knew his name.

The man, who looked vaguely familiar, leaned closer. "You ought to be more careful. Asking questions about Blue Fire booze ain't healthy."

"Why is that? It's just booze, isn't it?"

"It's the highest grade stuff sold around here, but that's not the issue. Word *is* the distribution is part of a vast network that's worth a lot of lolly to someone who doesn't want the details talked about."

"I get your drift. Say, who are you?"

"You don't need to know," said the skinny fella. "But I suggest you and your sheba quit askin' questions and go home where you belong." He followed this suggestion with a hard stare that made shivers run down Ben's back.

"But can you tell me..."

"Enough!" cried the man. He put down his nearly empty glass, slapped a bill on the table and limped out the door.

Ben returned to their table, carrying the peanuts and thinking furiously.

"Who was that?" said Anna.

"Don't know," Ben said. "But he warned me off asking questions about the Blue Fire products. Said 'It ain't healthy.'"

Anna stared. "Yikes. This isn't fun anymore. Your house has already been robbed and your father shot. Now this."

"Yeah. I know, it's a little scary. I guess that means I need to watch my back."

"I've had enough for one night. Let's ankle."

Chapter Seventeen

Over the next several evenings, Doc Junker and Tommy Crouch made the rounds of speakeasies and roadhouses in a rough circle around Big Grove, from Danville in the east to Mahomet on the west. Now they were headed out again.

"Hold your horses, Tommy. We're going off the main road now and there will be some serious potholes."

"We're lucky we have as many paved roads as we do," Tommy said. "Lots of little towns around here are still fighting mud. I can't tell you how many times I've been stuck out in the middle of nowhere."

Doc Junker planned to use this leg of the trip to Nine Gal Tavern in Mahomet to engage Tommy in casual chitchat and try to figure out what was eating him. He bided his time, knowing Tommy was more likely to talk in a smoky dive with other people partying around them than in the enforced intimacy of the Tin Lizzie.

Nine Gal Tavern was named after the original owners, the Bryants, who'd had nine red-haired daughters. The tavern was famous for its rowdy parties and for the fact that Abraham Lincoln had once stayed there. Now run by a relative of Gerald Cunningham's, it was located on Bloomington Road about one mile east of Mahomet.

They had arrived. Doc Junker turned the Model-T into a muddy side yard where a number of other Fords and Pathfinders lurked. Together, they mounted the rickety wooden steps and entered the front hall of the old farmhouse.

113

The wallpaper printed with hunting scenes harked back to the building's original appearance, but the partition between the front parlor and the dining room had been demolished to make one large apartment. This was crammed to the gills with furniture: end tables and armchairs, wingbacks and coffee tables. The original Turkish carpets and draperies still graced the floor and walls, and the light fixtures were converted gas sconces. At first glance, it looked like an overcrowded living room for a large family, but patrons clutching glasses and sitting on every available surface dispelled the illusion.

Doc Junker, who had visited the establishment years ago, remembered that the second floor boasted a billiards hall, a clever conversion from the nine Bryant daughters' dormitory-style bedroom. From the traffic streaming up and down the main staircase and the thump of feet above his head, he guessed it still had a billiards table and that the bar was upstairs. How would it be disguised this time? A cupboard, an upright piano, a niche in the wall with a false door?

He and Tommy ambled up the stairs and entered a crowded room that reeked of smoke and too many unwashed bodies. Aha! The bar area was the back half of a clothes closet with a rack of clothes at the ready to pull across and hide the liquor. Clever.

Tommy chose a table along the back wall while Doc Junker fetched their tipples. This time, he asked for gin and ice, and was startled to see the bottle from which the bartender poured was labeled "Blue Ruin." How appropriate. He squinted at the design on the label and recognized the Big Blue Stem grasses and the small print for "Blue Fire Distributors."

Doc Junker leaned on the bar, a backless bookcase on wheels that stored pairs of neatly aligned shoes on one side and bottles on the other. Glancing around, he noticed mostly men, dressed in everything from farm overalls to suits and dusters. Women were scarce, and the ones present were middle-aged and dressed in long-sleeved twinsets and skirts rather than eveningwear.

"Interesting clientele you have here," he said to the short, rotund barkeeper whose snub nose and curly hair identified him as a Cunningham.

The bartender laughed. "Yup, we get all kinds here. Local farmers, townies, people passing through on their way to Peoria—say, haven't I seen you before?"

"Illinois Junker, at your service. I'm a friend of Gerry Cunningham's."

"Thought so! I'm Leo, Gerry's nephew on his sister's side." Leo's round face split in a wide grin. "Here's your poison. That'll be one-fifty."

"Thanks, Leo." Doc Junker reflected he'd be broke pretty soon if he did too much of this kind of research—a shot of whiskey had gone from five cents to fifty cents as soon as Prohibition kicked in. He picked up the two drinks and a plate of nuts and navigated the crowded tables to Tommy's chosen perch.

Tommy's face showed no expression and his eyes were shadowed. That was a bad sign for someone who was normally so cheerful and outgoing. Doc Junker passed Tommy his drink and watched in dismay as he downed half of it in one gulp. No need for small talk, then.

"Tommy, I hear you've been thoroughly spifflicated on more than one occasion lately."

Tommy scowled and refused to meet Doc's eyes. He ran his fingers through his straight dark hair and scraped his chair back.

"Tommy?"

"Yeah, I've been drinking a tad more lately; what of it?"

Doc Junker looked at his associate. When had Tommy started going gray? Surely those silver threads on his head had just sprouted? Doc Junker felt a pang of guilt at how much he may have missed about Tommy's state of mind.

"Come on, Tommy. Something's bothering you. Tell me—whatever it is, I won't hold it against you." Doc Junker realized he was lying—if Tommy got himself involved the wrong way with Anna, he'd have plenty to say about it. But Tommy Crouch was one of his oldest friends—they'd served together in the Great War and Tommy had saved Doc's life by hauling him to safety after he was hit with shrapnel while crossing a field.

"You won't understand, Illinois."

Here we go, thought Doc Junker. "Try me."

Tommy sighed. He swallowed a couple of peanuts. "You'll think I'm some sap, not being able to handle this. You're so calm, you never let stuff upset you." His gaze locked onto Doc's for the first time.

Doc Junker cringed at the misery he saw in Tommy's green eyes. "Bushwa. Is that what you think? Believe me, I have plenty of bad moments. Maybe I'm just better at hiding my feelings than I used to be."

"Yeah, I guess a poker face like yours would be an asset for a physician. Then your patients can't guess what you're thinking until you decide to tell them."

Doc decided to take a leap. "Martha thinks you're unhappy in love."

Tommy actually chuckled. "If only it were that simple! Who does she think I'm stuck on?"

"Anna."

"What! Oh, no, it's not that way at all! Anna is a doll, but she's too young for me. I feel really protective about her, though. Don't like all of her friends."

"Well, I don't either, and I appreciate the number of times you've kept an eye on Anna. So what is it?"

Tommy blurted, "I'm having nightmares—about the war. I've been wondering if I'm going mad... I see mud, and shrapnel, and piece of bodies flying about..." He buried his head in his hands.

Instantly Doc Junker flashed back to one of his own nightmares and the roadhouse faded away...

...He tore around the corner of the trench, skidding in the stinking mud as artillery shots thudded overhead. The injured man was lying in the muck, screaming and holding his middle while icy rain soaked his clothes.

Dropping to his knees, Illinois pulled up the guy's bloody shirt. Stomach wound and uncontrollable bleeding. This fella was a goner, but he could offer pain relief. He pushed the wet hair and water out of his eyes with one grimy hand and groped for morphine in his medicine

116

satchel with the other.

The morphine bottle melted in his hand and the satchel disappeared.

Wump! Another shell exploded almost on top of them.

As both the dying man's screaming and the pounding overhead increased, the walls of the trench collapsed, burying them with dirt, rocks, water, and the wooden timbers used to shore up the sides.

Illinois gasped for air but inhaled mud. He was drowning in mud thousands of miles from home...

...someone jolted his chair, and Doc Junker rubbed his eyes with relief. No need for Tommy to tell him what it was like; he knew. Knew how the nightmare could blend into a daylight horror so time itself was all balled up. And it was in the trenches he'd first been called "Illinois" to differentiate him from all the other poor saps from Missouri and Iowa and all over.

And his legacy from that time was a bad leg and crippling depression every time he lost a patient...

Junker grabbed Tommy's hand. "Tommy, I have those nightmares too. I wake up pouring with sweat. Sometimes I don't sleep properly for a week. And the bad dreams come back each time I lose a patient."

Tommy stared, his Adam's apple jumping. "You do? But I thought you were so put together, so in control...I never would have guessed."

Doc Junker held his friend's trembling hand even tighter. "You thought you were alone? I can't even remember how many guys I've treated for shellshock since we got back. I have a sleeping powder that will help—but you shouldn't mix it with hooch."

Tommy shoved his glass away. "I won't take another drop if I can try the powder tonight. I'd give my soul for a single night of dreamless sleep."

"I'll get you a powder at my office on the way home," Junker promised. He sat back and sipped his drink, relieved now that he knew what had been bothering Tommy. Half his male patients either had shellshock or booze problems; often the two went together.

Loud laughter erupted off to his right. Turning, Doc Junker locked eyes with Bruce Donaldson.

Uh oh. Big Bruce was coming their way, glass in hand.

"Illinois Junker! Why is it I keep seeing you in drinking establishments?" He thrust his face closer to Junker, breathing whiskey fumes on him.

"I enjoy a drink, same as the next man."

"Oh, really? Say, I hear you and Crouch here want to know more about Blue Fire products. Just what is your interest?"

"Well, Donaldson. I don't know that it's really any of your business..."

Bruce pulled up a chair and thumped down on it. "Try me. Maybe I can enlighten you."

Junker thought fast. His father always said that telling as much of the truth as possible was always a good idea—less to remember that way. "A few of my patients are over-consuming hooch and sometimes mixing it with their meds, leading to serious problems. I've seen people get really sick or comatose and I'd like to find out where they get their white lightening and panther breath. This Blue Fire stuff seems to be everywhere, readily available."

Donaldson gave a crooked grin. "Think you're gonna stop people imbibing? Think again!" He took a slug of whiskey.

"Not stop them—slow them down a bit, maybe, and make my patients more aware of the bad things that can happen to their bodies when they mix my medicines with stuff containing chemicals or cocaine or goodness knows what."

"Huh," said Bruce. "Well, Blue Fire's local, that's for sure, but I don't rightly know who produces the stuff. I do know how it's transported, though." He winked at Tommy.

"How?" Doc Junker was interested in spite of himself. And he couldn't help wondering, why was Big Bruce being so helpful?

A couple of other men strolled up behind Donaldson, eager to hear what he had to say.

Bruce said, "For starters, there's the false-bottomed truck— you know, a load of wood or coal on a painted bed with a compartment underneath, where cases of booze are hidden.

Usually you see a decoy motorcar, just ahead or behind…"

"…to draw the excise agents, that's right," said a tall man in a fedora. "The decoy driver acts suspicious so he gets followed, and the truck with the booze sails right on through."

"Yup. Then there's false floorboards in the front of a car and false-bottomed shopping baskets for the ladies. Or the phony labeling trick: hooch in plain sight, but in opaque bottles labeled 'Buttermilk,' or 'Apple Juice.'"

"That's a good one!" The same man laughed.

Tommy pitched in. "Don't forget the skirt with a 'baby.' A sexy young woman can carry a pretty large bottle in her lap if it's bundled up like a child. The agents look at her smile and her bubs, not the 'baby.' I knew a man who crossed state lines that way."

"Yeah, and there's always room for a few more 'babies' in the boot," Big Bruce added.

"What about the flasks that flappers carry in their garters?" called a man at the back of the crowd. "Or in carriers strapped to their skinny waists under long coats?"

"Oh, those smart young things!" another man sniggered.

The conversation continued, getting more raucous as men imbibed while embroidering their tales. No one seemed worried that there might be an undercover excise agent listening. Doc Junker hadn't heard the bottle-dressed-as-a-baby story, but he knew most of the other methods of transport—Harry Stipes had seen to that. He wondered if Bruce Donaldson was speaking from personal experience. How did the Blue Fire Distributors move booze around central Illinois? And was Bruce involved? He decided to push for more information.

"What about home remedies with high alcohol content? How are they distributed?" he asked.

Big Bruce frowned. "Well, some are sold in pharmacies, right along with prescription medicines."

"Yeah," said the man with the fedora. "Last time I was into Jake's Drugs, I saw Jamaica Ginger right next to Finnish Blood Cleaner."

"Blood cleaner, eh?" Bruce guffawed. "Coffin varnish, more likely. And don't forget that door-to-door salesmen carry the stuff."

"There's another great product out there," said Tommy. "It's called Hinkley's Bone Liniment, and I heard that it's 90% alcohol. What I heard is probably true, since one of the proprietors described it as 'highly explosive to the innards.'"

"Sounds like jackass brandy—that stuff from Virginia made from peaches that causes internal bleeding," said a short fat man behind Bruce.

Doc Junker groaned. "See what I'm up against? If my patients down stuff like that, plus something with cocaine or morphine in it..."

"So what are you going to do about it?" Donaldson asked abruptly.

"Mind my own business, for the moment," Doc Junker replied. "Time to go, Tommy."

Chapter Eighteen
Same evening

Kelly's Roadhouse was hopping tonight.

Martha, knowing her husband and daughter were off gallivanting, had agreed to work this evening, her third night as a barmaid at an old barn turned roadhouse on the Mahomet side of town. To her surprise, she'd been hired on the spot when she presented herself to the harassed owner, John Gregory.

"You're the cat's pajamas as far as I'm concerned," he said to Martha. "Two of my girls have quit in the last week, and frankly I wouldn't care if you were seventy-five as long as you could serve set-ups and drinks. Pardon me, ma'am—no slight intended. It's just that I'm desperate."

"That's okay, Mr. Gregory. My four children are getting older, and they need so much. I could use the extra income." That was the truth but not the whole truth. It was Martha's habit to tell only as much as the current situation required. Years of navigating the complicated emotions of an immigrant family had taught her how to leave out inconvenient information when talking with her relations, especially the Texas part of the family. What they didn't know couldn't hurt you, so what you had to reveal should be kept as uninformative as possible. That way, you faced fewer criticisms from your nearest and dearest about your politics, your brand of religion, and how you raised your children. The same caution helped her deal with nosy neighbors as well.

Martha wiped off the tray she was carrying before loading it with glasses, a pint of Blue Fire whiskey, and a tray of cut lemons for delivery to the gentleman at the back table.

She was pleasantly surprised how much she enjoyed the work and the atmosphere. After years of assuming that roadhouses and speaks were squalid dens of iniquity, she found Kelly's a revelation. It was so ordinary. A converted barn, the juice joint was a cheerful, bustling place that was clean and remarkably comfortable with a variety of seating options for patrons of different ages: padded benches, booths, round tables, and rectangular tables with oilcloth covers.

There were more women than she'd expected. Middle-aged women, dressed like Martha in long skirts and blouses or twinsets, out with their husbands for a little fun, occupied the tables and the corner booths, while the young people perched close together on high stools at the bar. Although one or two men were clearly bent on getting pickled, everyone else seemed to have their drinking under control. Older women frequently chose cider or lemonade, or cocktails with a fruit juice base and lots of sugar.

Tray loaded, she carried it to the patron. "That will be two-fifty, sir."

"Aw, that's highway robbery!" complained the man.

"Sir, you requested Canadian whiskey—that costs more than the gallon goods."

Grousing, the man groped in his pocket and passed her a ten. Martha made change for him and headed back to the bar.

Someone changed the radio station and the mellow tones of Bessie Smith poured out into the room. Martha collected her next order, including a dish of nuts, and took it to a booth full of young men and girls who were certainly enjoying themselves. One young man with slicked-back, parted hair like Rudolph Valentino actually winked at her. Martha felt a pleasant glow in her cheeks and was glad she'd worn her new sweater that brought out the blue of her eyes.

"Martha!" the bartender yelled. "Next order up!"

She picked up her pace, reflecting that a few evenings on her feet like this would either toughen her up or exhaust her completely. At least she was accomplishing her mission: Martha had already swiped a couple of Blue Fire bottles from the trash when no one was looking and stuffed them into her capacious handbag. And, she had a pretty good idea where Mr. Gregory kept his liquor receipts.

The evening progressed without incident, until about nine-thirty when Martha turned around with a loaded tray and saw a familiar face.

Her husband Earl was staring at her from the doorway. Since he was fully garbed in hat and overcoat, it was clear he had just entered the roadhouse.

Martha clutched her tray. If she hadn't been so startled, she would have enjoyed the utterly baffled look on his face. His eyebrows shot up and his lips disappeared into his beard.

Martha shook her head slightly at him and glided over. "Would you like a table, sir? I see a free one at the back."

Earl and Tommy Crouch followed her, Tommy looking very confused.

Doc Junker hissed at his wife. "What in tarnation are you doing here? I've never seen you set foot in one of these joints!"

"I will the whole story tell you later," she whispered, as she set down her tray and pulled out an order pad. "The short answer is I do research for the WCTU. I am undercover." Then, in a louder voice, "What will you have, sir? Beer, gin, whiskey, cocktail-of-the-day, or a set-up?"

Martha's husband scratched his head vigorously, as if he had lice, and smiled ruefully. "A small whiskey, please, ma'am. And my friend here will have a lemonade."

Tommy gazed at Martha as if he'd never seen her before. Then his face split in a grin of sheer admiration. "A tall lemonade would be swell, thanks."

Junker was stunned. His Martha serving drinks and set-ups in a speakeasy! A public drinking hall where friends and neighbors could see her doing it! He couldn't believe she could have such a change of heart after so many years of condemning hooch and all those who imbibed.

Maybe the Woman's Christian Temperance Union wasn't such a bad thing if it made Martha Huber Junker look at the world in a new way. He was pretty sure her mission was to control or shut down the illegal distribution of alcohol; oddly, that put them on the same side of the fence for a change.

Junker smiled as he paid his barmaid/wife for the whiskey and lemonade. Watching her swish around the room as if she were born to it, he thought he'd never seen her look prettier. Her face was alive with interest and her cheeks were pink. Maybe, just maybe, this little adventure meant he could persuade her to accompany him sometimes for an evening out—like the other middle-aged couples he saw enjoying themselves around the room.

And, if he were really lucky, the sheer excitement of doing something new and attracting attention to herself would get Martha in the mood for other things...

A man can hope.

Chapter Nineteen
Wednesday afternoon

A few days later, the speakeasy team met in the lounge of the Inman Hotel, an eight-year-old hotel boasting steam heat, electricity, and a hairdresser on call. The room was furnished with wingback chairs, Turkish carpets, and delicate round tables. Carefully placed vases of fresh flowers and linen napkins created a posh atmosphere. It smelled of cigarette smoke and expensive perfume.

Anna thought it was the most elegant hotel in Big Grove. She pretended that she wasn't a girl out with her father and boyfriend; instead she was a wealthy matron from Chicago, about to have cocktails with important friends. In her daydream, she wore an expensive wool velour suit, a beaver-fur stole, and a darling tilt-brimmed hat with a huge feather that dropped becomingly over her right shoulder. Her patent leather Lorraine shoes were brand new.

"Anna!" hissed Ben. "The waiter wants to know what'll you'll have to drink."

"A cranberry sling," Anna said without thinking.

"Not at this time of day," said Doc Junker. "Hot cocoa with whipped cream for the young lady and hot tea for me. Ben? Tommy?"

Doc Junker had chosen easy chairs arranged in a small circle in an alcove so they wouldn't be overheard. Anna had made the mistake of sitting near the window, which meant a chilly draft swirled around her thin stockings. Too bad the beaver stole was imaginary.

Off to her right, she could see Westside Park looking very uninviting with its coating of snow under gray skies. What would it be like to live in the south? Balmy temperatures, flowers all year around...

"Anna!"

"Sorry, Papa. I was daydreaming. So, we're reporting our speakeasy findings?"

"Yes. Tommy and I did the rounds of roadhouses outside Big Grove. Not much to report, except a very interesting encounter with Big Bruce Donaldson." He described the conversation.

Ben said, "Sounds almost like he was trying to distract you with good humor, Doc. Pull the wool over your eyes by being unnecessarily helpful."

"Exactly what I thought," said Doc Junker with a sharp nod of approval.

Tommy leaned forward, his hands clasped between his knees. "He seems to know an awful lot about how hooch is transported around Illinois."

"Yes, but that's not proof he's involved," Anna said. She noticed that Tommy's color was better today, almost as if he'd spent the night sleeping in a bed instead of at a speak nodding over a bottomless glass.

"He is still our most likely big cheese," Doc Junker replied. "But an operation of the scale we suspect could never be accomplished by one man working alone. He must have employees."

"My money's on young Donaldson, the nephew," said Tommy. "As an employee—not the big cheese."

Ben winced. "Frank is my friend, but I think you are probably right. He keeps cropping up in the wrong place at the wrong time. It's hard to believe he's innocent."

"It's not just the people we need to pin down," said Doc Junker. "Before the police get involved, we need to identify at least one location where the gang is warehousing their products."

"Like Tate Farm. Surely it's no accident that I found all those invoices out there."

"I agree, Ben, but there's probably at least one more drop-off or storage facility nearby. Like someplace in downtown Big Grove. We're talking about a large volume of Blue Fire products—not just the whiskey and gin, but the home remedies."

"So how are we going to find those places?" asked Ben. "Spy on the principals?"

Doc Junker said, "Yup. Keep a close eye on the key players: Big Bruce Donaldson, his nephew Frank, and anyone else who seems to be spending a lot of time in their company."

Ben nodded. "I can track Frank. I see a lot of him anyhow."

Anna giggled. "That means you're a suspect, Ben."

Ben rolled his eyes as the waiter hurried by bearing a platter of hot sandwiches. As the rich scent of roast beef and fried onions reached Anna's nostrils, she discovered she was ravenous. Would her father order a snack for them, even though it was only two hours before dinnertime?

Doc Junker had his mind on other things. "Tommy and I will work out a plan for following Big Bruce. What we need is to catch him red-handed transporting or selling hooch or alcoholic home remedies to individuals. I also have a young friend on the police force who will help as much as he can without getting in trouble with his boss..."

"Doc, you mean Graziano Fellini and his boss Han the Hun, don't you?" said Tommy.

"Yes, of course I do. Fellini is a master of disguise—he can go anywhere. He has to find a delicate balance between investigations on his own and letting Han the Hun think he—Stoltman, I mean—is on top of everything going on."

"Like sitting on the edge of a razor," Tommy muttered.

Ben's eyebrows snapped together. "Would Fellini be a skinny guy who haunts speakeasies? I think I've already met him."

Doc Junker nodded. "Fellini's on our side, and I asked him to look out for you. That's because I don't want you two kids to tangle with the big crooks. They're dangerous, and I'm pretty sure they have gang contacts with Shelton down south or Capone in Chicago. We need to find out where they meet and then bring in the police to do the actual dirty work."

"This is so exciting!" Anna said with shining eyes.

Her father gave her a jaundiced look. "Now Anna, I know it's exciting, but you must keep in mind that bootleggers are nasty folk who won't hesitate to kill you if they think you are a threat to them. Don't forget Harry Stipes."

Anna wilted a little. "I know, Papa. But wait a minute, how are we going to spy on these men when some of them already know we're interested in their activities?"

The others looked at each other. Ben said, "Mix ourselves up and appear all casual-like in their favorite haunts?"

"Hmm," Doc Junker muttered. "I like that, Ben. We'll send out different combinations of the four of us—five counting Fellini—to speakeasies and restaurants we know the Donaldsons frequent. And I can recruit a couple more folks like Gerry Cunningham to help with tailing."

"Papa!" said Anna. "Sally just got her driver's license. She can drive her father's Model T and the two of us could…

"I'd rather you drove around with Ben or Tommy," said her father grimly.

"I'll be careful. I promise!" Anna said it half-heartedly; she knew when she was defeated.

"Famous last words," said Ben. "Doc, I promise you, I'll stick to Anna like glue and make sure she doesn't get into trouble."

"I'll hold you to that, Ben."

There was a commotion at the door leading into the lobby.

Steve Busey rushing in, his hair wild. His gaze swiveled around the room until he spotted Ben Keck.

"Ben! I've been looking everywhere for you!" He put a hand on Ben's shoulder.

"What is it, Steve? You're all of a lather."

"Frank Donaldson's been shot."

Chapter Twenty

Doc Junker drove Ben, Anna, and Steve Busey to Burnham hospital. Ben crouched in the front passenger seat, his face pale and his fists clenched.

Anna, slumped in the back seat next to Steve, tried not to dwell on what Steve had said. Shot in the chest—not much blood, but Frank was unresponsive when the ambulance took him away...

"Where did it happen, Steve?" Ben turned his head.

"The alley behind the Steamroom. Frank uses the back door a lot—whoever shot him knew that."

The Tin Lizzie pulled up in front of the emergency room. "Go on in," said Junker. "I'll park and join you as soon as I can."

Anna and the two young men jumped out. As soon as they entered the lobby, Anna's nose was assaulted with the familiar smells of carbolic and ether. Another more elusive scent, compiled from cold sweat and fear, hovered in corners with waiting relatives. She spotted the Donaldson family.

Frank's mother and two sisters huddled together in a corner, sobbing. Nathan Donaldson was nowhere to be seen—perhaps talking with the doctor? Anna's stomach roiled. She knew it was bad news.

Ben rushed over to Mrs. Donaldson.

"Ben!" she cried. "Oh, Ben, I'm glad you are here! You were such a good friend to Frank..." She grabbed his arm and pulled him close.

Steve put a hand under Anna's elbow and led her to a group of chairs on the side of the waiting room. "We'd better let them have some privacy," he whispered.

Anna nodded, surprised and grateful that Steve Busey was taking care of her. Before now, she'd seen him as a professional flirt and speakeasy habitué, one of the numerous men pursuing Sally McKinley. Yet he was a friend of both Frank and Ben— he must have some good qualities.

She watched with sinking heart as Ben listened to Mrs. Donaldson and bowed his head, shoulders shaking. That meant Frank was dead, then. How awful...to lose a son, a brother. Those poor sisters. Poor Ben. How could she comfort him without being smarmy?

Steve stood abruptly and went over to pay his respects. Anna had never met Mrs. Donaldson or the girls—Aileen and Barbara, she thought—and she hesitated. Surely they wouldn't want a girl they hardly knew expressing condolences?

Her father interrupted her uncomfortable thoughts by appearing at her side and placing a warm hand on her shoulder. "Let me see what I can do for the family," he said. "Wait here. I'll be back shortly."

But she didn't have to wait very long. When Steve sat down on the other side of Mrs. Donaldson, Ben stood and headed back to Anna. He slumped into the chair next to her, hands white-knuckled on his knees and eyes squeezed shut. His cheeks were wet.

Anna's heart ached. She discovered she didn't care how it looked, she just reached over and put both arms around Ben's unresisting body and hung on tight.

"Ben, I am so, so sorry."

He turned towards her and buried his face against her neck. "What filthy, rotten luck...just wait until I find out who did it." And he cried noisily, without reserve, and Anna patted his back and let her shirtwaist soak up his tears.

Chapter Twenty-one
Thursday afternoon

It was time. Martha found herself eager to hear from the other barmaids—mostly young things in their twenties, she suspected. She quaked a little at the thought of joining them at the podium. She grabbed her fox stole, slid her feet into wool-lined boots and waited near the front door for Jo to pick her up for the Women's Christian Temperance Union meeting.

"Ready for action?" asked Jo when Martha opened the car door.

The old Ford emitted smells of musty upholstery and stale tobacco from Gerry's pipe. Martha lowered herself into the front seat, wincing at the frigid air swirling around her. A few snowflakes settled on the shoulders of her winter coat.

"What kind of action? Aren't we just going to hear the reports of the bargirls?" She wondered what the others would say when she'd given her own report—no one in the WCTU except Jo knew Martha was one of the barmaids. And Cora Busey would no doubt be scandalized and be very vocal about it to anyone who would listen. Martha couldn't forget that Cora had voted against Martha being accepted into the WCTU because she was a "beer-guzzling German."

"Yes, but we have to plan what to do next!" Jo lifted both hands off the wheel as she gesticulated, making Martha even more nervous. The automobile careened around the corner of Elm and Green streets.

"Careful, Jo! You'll have us off the road if you keep driving like that."

"Sorry. I'm just so excited that the WCTU is finally doing something substantive about illegal booze. And I can't wait to hear your report, Martha dear. I still can't believe you actually took that job at Kelly's."

"Well, we haven't done anything yet except collect information," Martha said. "And as for taking the job, it seemed like the right thing to do." And, she remembered with a small shock, she'd actually enjoyed the work.

"Yes, but this is the beginning of making a difference. If we can shut down the folks who are distributing the hooch, our speakeasies might be pleasanter places to visit—for women, too. Why, I might even go if I knew I could meet my friends there and have something besides alcohol!"

With a flash of understanding, Martha recalled what Earl had always said—that people would drink no matter what. And if the WCTU closed off one source of booze, others would open up. Hadn't she seen it in her own family? Her father had always found another stash of liquor when one dried up—just as he always found a new hiding place for his bottles when his wife cleaned them out. And Earl and Anna, they both had the habit. If one speak was shuttered, another would appear like toadstools popping up after a rain. At least mushrooms were useful; Martha grew edible mushrooms in the basement and knew how to weed out poisonous types when she collected edible plants in Busey Woods... She shook herself. Now was not the time to let her mind wander.

They arrived in one piece, despite Jo's erratic driving. A buzz of excitement met them in the cloakroom. Women poured in, hanging their coats, shedding boots, and checking their hair in the ornately framed long mirror.

"Well, Jo!" Cora Busey said. "I suppose today is the day we find out how efficient our snooping operation is!"

"Not snooping, Cora—legitimate research on illegal alcohol sales in Champaign County," said Jo stiffly.

"Women are good at gossiping, so it stands to reason they'd be good at ferreting out scandalous behavior," said another woman Martha did not recognize.

Snooping, in other words, thought Martha.

"Where's Karin Keillor?" Cora asked. "I can't wait to hear from her again—she seems to know what's going on. Even if she is a foreigner."

Martha was tempted to slap Cora.

"Don't you wish you'd decided to be a barmaid, Cora?" Gretchen McKinley asked. "You have the acting ability and the courage. You'd be a natural."

"Me!" said Cora, turning pink at the very idea. "My husband would never let me hear the end of it! Oh, my hair is a mess!" She patted her Marcel Wave back into submission.

Martha smiled. If they only knew! Not only had she, the "beer-guzzling German," worked as a barmaid, but her husband had caught her in the act. When they'd discussed her new job, Earl's reaction had displayed a comical mixture of horror and admiration, mixed with fear for her safety.

"*Lieblinge*, now that I've told you the truth about what happened to Stipes, you do understand the danger, don't you? Someone poisoned him to shut his mouth, and that someone probably has something to do with Blue Fire Distributors."

"Yes, Earl, but I must go back one more time and try to get some receipts for the WCTU. I promised myself, and I want to make a success. Besides, these bootleggers don't even know who I am."

Junker sighed. "I won't say you can't go, as much as I would like to..."

"You will not stop me! When can I ever stop you from doing what you mean to do, even dangerous things?" She knew he couldn't argue with that.

Junker reluctantly said she could go back to work one more time, and that she could tell the Union she was a barmaid. But the story of Stipes was strictly out of bounds until the murderer was caught. Martha agreed, shivering. She had no desire to meddle with murder...

Now Martha trooped up the wide staircase with the others. In short order, Jo Cunningham had them seated and called the meeting to order.

"Ladies, we've only been on the job for a fortnight, but I thought we should pool our findings so far so we know better what to look for. And remember, no reports go outside this room—not even to your husbands. We don't want anyone to get into trouble. Who would like to go first?"

A tall redhead came forward.

"I'm Mary Stoltmann," she said. Mary was a buxom thirty-year-old housewife with two children in primary school. "After I found a babysitter for Clea and Jackie, I approached several speakeasies until I found a vacancy at a new speak on Randolph St. It's called Casey's. I haven't been able to pinch any receipts because my boss is always looking over my shoulder, but I write notes in the powder room whenever I can about what I've seen." She spread out a grubby piece of paper on the podium. "Most of the hooch is labeled either 'Blue Fire Distributors' or 'Peoria Bottling Company.' I don't know who my boss buys from, but I did overhear him refer to a 'Mr. D.'"

Karin Keillor was next. "My brother and I have swiped some receipts, and there seems to be a pattern. As Mary said, the booze comes from the Blue Fire or Peoria Bottling companies, and also from Chicago—an outfit called 'Windy City Liquors.' We don't know who sells it to our bartenders, but we do know how it arrives." She paused and caught the eye of a friend in the second row. "It comes by truck, late at night, disguised as a load of Coca-Cola."

Sensation. Everyone wanted to know how Karin had obtained that information. Martha leaned forward as Karin described how her brother hid himself in a storeroom overnight at the Cat's Pajamas and watched the unloading of the shipment. The cola bottles lay in a double layer over the cases of hooch.

Martha was fascinated. She couldn't remember feeling this gripped by a topic, a quest, since the beginning of nursing school when she hunted through the literature for cures for whooping cough. Housekeeping and cooking just didn't produce the same drive to know, to find out how and when and what.

The assembly listened to several more reports that revealed nothing new beside what they'd already heard.

Jo waited until the comments died down and women started

looking around expectantly. "I think we have one more report that will interest all of you," Jo announced with a hint of triumph.

Martha stood up. Behind her, someone gasped. As she walked to the podium, she heard rustles and waves of whispers: "It's Martha Junker, the doctor's wife!"

And, "it's that German woman!"

She gripped the sides of the podium with both hands. She gazed at the startled but avid faces of women who thought they knew her and took a deep breath. "I decided I could not at home stay. I went to Kelly's Roadhouse, on the edge of town, and took a job as a barmaid. The owner, Mr. Gregory was desperate for a replacement server, and he did not care that I am over his age. I see many Blue Fire bottles, and the Peoria Bottling Company label, also."

Martha paused to take another breath; she wasn't accustomed to public speaking. The room was completely silent. "Then my husband walks in to the roadhouse. You may imagine his surprise!" Several gasps and an outright giggle from somewhere to the left gave her courage to go on. "I pretend I do not know him and serve him whiskey."

"What happened when you got home, Martha?"

"Did your husband forbid you to go back?"

"How could you do it, you, a doctor's wife!" That was Cora, naturally.

Martha removed her hands from their death grip on the podium. "My husband supports me in this job. It is fine for me to continue."

A storm of applause. Jo Cunningham clapped the loudest.

"Well, Martha! Now you are one of our warriors!" she said with a broad grin.

Martha discovered her knees felt wobbly from all the excitement. The buzz of comments and questions lasted all the way back to her seat.

"Okay, ladies! Now for the actions items: how long shall we collect evidence, and what shall we do with it when we stop?" Jo asked the group.

"I say at least another two weeks," said Karin. "It's hard to get a feeling for how a place operates until you spend several weeks working there."

The other women agreed to that.

"Then what?" Jo said.

Martha raised her hand. "My husband, Doctor Junker, knows a policeman who can be trusted. Let us take the collected evidence to him."

The suggestion passed and the meeting adjourned at four-thirty.

Chapter Twenty-Two

That very evening, Martha reported to Kelly's at six for another stint as a barmaid. She spotted her boss (Mr. Gregory to his face, "Grig" as his employees referred to him) passing the cloakroom.

"Hello, Mr. Gregory!" she said as she hung up her coat and put on her server's apron.

"Evening, Mrs. Junker. We have a lot of customers tonight, so hop to it!" He looked harried and his hair—what there was of it—was standing on end.

"Yes, sir." Martha changed her boots for sturdy shoes since she would be on her feet for hours and checked to make sure she had pad and pen in her apron pocket.

After her conversation two nights ago with Earl, she was determined to complete her mission sooner rather than later. Her husband had warned her that what she was doing could be dangerous; he wanted her out of there as soon as possible. She had to grab some physical evidence, preferably some receipts for liquor purchase with incriminating additions like names and dates. Then she could vanish from the scene and leave the field to the younger women working at other speakeasies and roadhouses.

She wiped the counter with a clean cloth, scooping up spilled hooch and water left from condensate. Her tray stood ready for the next order, but her hand shook a little as she centered it. Martha Huber Junker—a staunch Lutheran, wife, and mother—a lawbreaker? What she was contemplating was theft, pure and simple. Stealing her boss's paperwork. True, if she were caught, the worst that would probably happen was that she'd get fired, but for someone used to doing everything church and society expected of a proper, God-fearing woman, the whole idea upset her. She was in the odd position of being shocked at her own behavior...even before she behaved badly.

A customer across the room lifted his hand and Martha nodded. She picked up her pad and sallied forth to collect his order.

"Gentlemen, what can I get you?" Three men in suits and fedoras eyed her from their tilted-back chairs. Just like Earl, she thought—always risking the furniture.

One man brought his chair down with a crash that made Martha wince. "Set-up with lemon and soda water for me," he said.

"Gin-and-ice, and a whiskey straight up," said the tall thin one, who appeared to be speaking for his shorter companion. "And make it snappy, ma'am. We have business to settle and then we have to move along."

"Of course," Martha said smoothly. Some folks were always in a hurry. She was getting used to all kinds of manners, and the slogan "we are here to serve the customer" was posted in the back hallway in case she or the other servers forgot who was really in charge here. Money talked, and buyers didn't have to be polite as long as they produced cash.

The jazz pianist started up with a rolled chord and then a rollicking tune, one Martha did not recognize. She liked it though, and smiled at the young piano player as she passed him. This earned her a wink and a flip of his bangs, which were not slicked back like most of the male customers.

She plunked her tray on the counter, saw there were no more order slips, and decided to visit the powder room while she could. This took her down the back hallway, passing her boss's office.

Martha had been inside Grig's office just twice, once when she interviewed for the position and the other time when she had a question about payday. He was almost always there, lurking behind his big desk, sorting papers and signing receipts.

Today, however, his normally locked strongbox stood open on a side table and the office was empty.

She didn't hesitate. With a quick glance both ways to see that no one observed her, Martha nipped in, slipped her hand into the box of receipts and documents and grabbed the bottom quarter without even looking at it. She shoved the pile into the capacious pocket of her serving apron and slid out the door.

Grig might notice that his pile was slightly shorter, but perhaps not. It was an untidy stack, and if she were lucky, he wouldn't notice that he was missing some receipts until later. The thing to do now was to cut short her normal four-hour shift and vanish. She could invent an emergency at home and pretend she'd heard from one of her children. Maybe one of the twins had set the house on fire? No, too obvious. How about her youngest throwing up while her husband was out on a childbirth call? Better. But there was only one phone at Kelly's—ah! She had it! She'd call home to check on her transport and pretend to be called away.

Martha hurried into the powder room. She locked herself in a stall and took several deep, slow breaths to calm the drumming of her heart. Clearly, a life of crime was not for her—Earl said she had a lousy poker face, and she knew her hands were trembling. She closed the lid of the toilet, sat down, and fished out the handful of receipts.

"Oct 30, 3 cs Canadian wsky, Peoria Bt.... Peoria Bottling Company."

"Received, Nov. 3, two cs Blue Fire whiskey, 1 cs gin, from M. D...." Who was M.D.? Maybe Earl would know.

"Rec'vd Oct 27, 4 bts brandy and 3 barrels near beer, B.F. fr xxx" The last word was blurred so Martha couldn't read it.

"Near beer" was the watered down version of real beer—supposedly with less alcohol. The other servers had told Martha that near beer tasted like barley water, but it was cheaper than whiskey or gin.

Most of the receipts were signed by Mr. Gregory, a few by the assistant manager Marvin Garvey. She examined the wad of paper left in her hand in the dim light that filtered into her stall. Unfolding it, she skimmed the handwritten notes: "local 'leggers…homemade labels…brisk trade in tonics…Blue Fire Dst.…." Clearly this was something Earl should see. But who had written it?

"Martha! You're needed out front! Hustle a bit, honey!"

"Coming, Angie!" Martha called. Angie was almost fifty, the most experienced of the servers, and happy to take new employees under her wing.

She stuffed the receipts and notes inside her brassiere—she didn't want to chance pulling out the wrong papers from her apron when she made up the tabs. She straightened her clothing and opened the stall door. A little cold water on her face would restore her equilibrium.

Feeling calmer, Martha decided to work another half an hour and then call home and fake receiving the news that would allow her to leave early. By the time Grig figured out she'd been lying—if he ever did—she'd be long gone. Martha wasn't planning to work after tonight.

But it didn't work out quite the way she'd hoped. The first fifteen minutes passed without incident, and Martha actually caught herself thinking she would miss the stimulation of this job. The bustle and the cheerful chat, and the fun of looking at everyone's clothing and guessing at their relationships as they arrived in duos and quartets. Then, just as she filled an order for two gents and a lady at the bar who wanted cranberry slings with whiskey instead of gin, she heard a roar from the back.

"Goddamn it, someone's been in my strongbox!"

Grig had discovered the theft and was on the warpath!

Martha's skin crawled and beads of sweat gathered under her twin set as she endeavored to act as if the cry meant nothing to her and move normally. How was she going to get out of here before Grig questioned all the staff?

"Angie! Get back here!" shouted the boss.

Angie disappeared down the hallway.

No time to waste. Martha rushed up to the bar. "Harry, may I use the phone? I need to check on my ride home."

"Sure, doll. Just don't tie it up very long, okay?"

She dialed.

Anna picked up. "Mama, I was about to call you. Emma is

140

throwing up all over the place and Papa isn't here yet. Can you come home early?"

"Give her a little ginger tea as soon as she'll take anything; there is some fresh root in the icebox. I'll be home as soon as I can."

She called Jo, and fortunately Jo was available to pick her up early.

Martha shivered as she realized her hypothetical excuse for leaving had become real. If she didn't believe in the infinite power of God, she might think she was a witch...*Danke, Gott.* She untied her apron and pulled on her coat.

As she hustled out the door, she heard Grig say, "Send Martha in, would you?"

Jo pulled up just in time and Martha yanked open the passenger door.

"How come the early departure, Martha?" she asked.

"I'll tell you on the way home. Just get us out of here!"

Doc Junker and his wife huddled over the kitchen table.

Martha spread out the receipts and notes she'd stolen from Kelly's.

Junker's eyes lit up. "Well done, *Lieblinge!*" He began sorting them by distributor or bottling company. Martha helped, creating four rows for "Blue Fire Distributing Co.," Peoria Bottling Co.," "Windy City Liquors," and "Other."

Junker was not surprised that the Blue Fire pile grew the fastest. "Hmm. They are selling whiskey, gin, brandy, beer, near-beer, and health tonics. Quite a little business."

Martha rose and fetched her shopping list pad and a pencil. "I'll start a list for the Peoria Bottling Co." That turned out to be mostly whiskey. So did the Windy City Liquors, but their sales included cases of Canadian bonded whiskey from over the Canadian border, probably through Wisconsin.

"But who is controlling the local sales?" muttered Junker. "That I could stand to know. Aha!" He pounced on the receipt with the initials M.D. "M.D...certainly not a physician. One of the Donaldson family? Can't be Nathan or Bruce or Frank...wait a minute! That letter is not an 'M,' it's an 'N!'

Dang, that means it's Nathan Donaldson!" He pounded the table with one fist. "Nathan, not Big Bruce, is the big cheese!"

"*Nathan*?" said his wife. "It does not seem possible! He is so scruffy, so stand-offish—I do not know what word to use."

"Not shy or retiring, that's for sure. Perhaps ornery, unpredictable, or smarmy. He may be a better actor than I've ever realized. Hmm. But where does Big Bruce come into it? I am sure he is involved somehow."

Martha rummaged through the Blue Fire pile. "I saw another receipt with the initials 'B. D.' in the signature area. Where is it? Ach! Here, look here."

Junker bent over it, squinting at the irregular writing. "Yep, Big Bruce it is. I know that big loopy B. Good work!"

"Look at this one, Earl. These are the notes of someone, perhaps for an article of some kind?" Martha fished out the wad of notes that had been at the bottom of the strongbox in Mr. Gregory's office.

Junker latched onto the handwriting immediately. "It looks like Harry's writing…"

"Harry Stipes, the man who took too much digitalis?"

"The same. My patient and good buddy. It makes sense; he told me about his interest in local bootlegging. I thought he might be writing an article on it, but I didn't have any proof." He jumped up from the table and paced around the kitchen. "Depending on how he went about it, his work could have proved dangerous if he mentioned names. A reporter could get caught in the middle—how to gather enough evidence to satisfy his editor without leading to arrests and retaliations from the bootleggers."

Martha stared at him. "But someone thought Stipes would give them away and so they poisoned him?"

"Exactly. But we still don't know who the murderer is. I will take these papers over to Fellini and maybe he can make some progress. *Liebling*, I am so glad I married a smart woman—saves having to explain everything twice and then some."

"Ach!" cried Martha. "All you Junker men have low opinion of the female brain. Just because we think in circles and not in line to point…"

"I think you mean, linearly, from Point A to Point B."

"Do not tell me what meaning have I! You know what I say!"

Doc Junker laughed. He did so enjoy getting her riled up and watching her skin flush pink. "You are the best of women, and I do understand what you are saying." He really wanted to take her upstairs, right then. Instead, he gave her a quick hug and a kiss and turned Harry's wad of notes over. Stipes had continued to write on the back side of the last page. "Liquor drops sch'ld eves Nov 7, 18, 26...Dec 2, 10, 15, 20...Tate Farm."

He stopped reading. Today was December twentieth. He would have to go out there.

Junker explained what he was thinking to Martha.

"But Earl, that is not smart! You know these men are dangerous!"

"That is why I am calling Officer Fellini first—he will arrange to meet me, with back-up. This could be our chance to crack this distribution ring and collect some hard evidence."

"I am not happy! I think you are being foolish—you just want to be in the middle!"

Junker took her hand. "Of course I want to be 'in the middle'! I want to see Harry avenged and put a stop to Blue Fire products being sold left, right, and center to my patients. The crap they sell is killing people."

Martha sighed and rose from the table. "I will go upstairs, then. But I will not sleep until you come home."

Chapter Twenty-three
Same evening

Anna crept away from the dining room where she'd been listening to her parents. Her father was going out to Tate Farm! She and Ben couldn't miss being in on the kill—not after all they'd done to help. Yes, it would be dangerous, but she and Ben would hang back out of the way and let the police do their jobs. Staying home just wasn't an option.

She could hear her father on the telephone now. "...Yes, an hour at the outside...I will meet you at the north edge, near the big barn...no, I know better than that, though I would dearly like to confront Nathan on my own..."

Anna waited behind the door to the living room until her father had collected his coat and hat. He exited through the kitchen door, closing the door softly. Then she ran for her own coat and crept out the front door as soon as she heard his car leave the shared driveway.

Ben's second-story window showed a faint light. Good—he was probably going through his photographs since there was another photography contest he wanted to enter. How was she going to attract his attention without disturbing his parents? It wasn't original, but she'd just have to throw gravel at his window. If she could throw that high.

Turned out her aim was terrible and the gravel from the driveway spattered all over the wooden clapboards of the first story. No response. She threw a second handful, and was rewarded by the clatter of pebbles against glass. Still no response. Anna seized a third handful of larger stones and used an underhand throw.

Crash. Then Ben's voice hissed through a just-opened window. "Stop it, you idiot! You've cracked the glass!"

"Sorry! But you've got to come. Get your coat and car keys. It's really urgent, Ben."

"Okay." Ben's head vanished from the square of light above her.

In a few minutes, he was beside her. "Tell me," he said as he grabbed her hand and headed for his father's Model-T.

Anna filled him in on what her parents had discovered from the liquor receipts and Stipes' notes. Ben stopped in mid-stride and stared. "You mother, who hates drinking establishments, was posing as a barmaid?"

"Yes. I'm really quite proud of her." Anna was also shocked, but Ben didn't need to know that. "She and my father don't usually work together on his causes. But this time, their interests overlapped. Mother's WCTU group is trying to stop the illegal sale of hooch in speakeasies; Papa wants to halt Blue Fire's distribution of dangerous tonics."

"Even if your father succeeds, putting Blue Fire Distributors out of business will only be a drop in the bucket. Other folks will continue to sell and transport booze in whatever way they can—until the Volstead Act is scrapped."

"I'm sure you're right, Ben. Oh, do hurry up! I'm worry about Papa going out there alone."

Ben struggled with the ignition, which coughed and died. He tried again, and his father's car started. "I'm really going to need my own vehicle soon," he muttered. "But right now, I can't afford it."

For most of the ride out to Tate Farm, Anna and Ben did not talk. Anna was reviewing what she knew about the bootleggers in her mind while Ben concentrated on driving fast but not too fast. "Ben," she said suddenly. "What if Dick Tate is out there tonight?"

"I almost hope he is," said Ben. "So I can drag him away and make him see how stupid he is to be involved with those thugs and to have led Frank astray the way he did."

"You don't think Dick had anything to do with the attack at

your house, do you?"

"No. But it could have been arranged by someone he knew. Or maybe one of the fellas from the bootlegging gang in southern Illinois."

They were close now. Ben pulled the car off the road well before the Tate Farm turnoff and slid it behind a large bush. He stopped the engine. "At least there is no moon tonight. And even better, it's not sleeting or snowing."

"Even so, it's freezing cold," said Anna as she fastened the buttons on her coat and jammed on her wool cloche. Someday, she thought, someone will invent a better coat for skulking around at night—this one had too many openings for cold air leaks.

"Okay," Ben said. "Let's not be stupid about this. We're going to investigate, but very, very quietly. And then if one of us gets caught, the other is going to run back and drive the car back to town and get help. I'm leaving the key just here, under the mat. Got it?"

"Yes. But I think Papa already called for police backup. Can't we just wait for them?"

"Don't count on the police arriving on time, especially with Han the Hun in charge. Hey, Anna—don't close your door all the way. Just pull it almost shut, like this."

She copied Ben and then followed him to the nearest barn, a few hundred yards from where Ben had parked his Ford. A side door let them into a dim interior full of crated bottles. Anna shivered as something rustled near the ceiling. Bats? Or doves?

Ben and Anna checked the contents of one of the open crates—Canadian whiskey—and they tiptoed towards the far end of the building where Anna could hear voices.

"...So, you thought you'd be a hero and put an end to our business, eh?" That was a voice she did not recognize. Then her father spoke.

"Well look what the cat dragged in! Nathan Donaldson! What are you doing out here at Tate? You oughtta..."

The rest of her father's speech was cut off by the revving of a truck engine.

Chapter Twenty-four
Same evening (a little earlier)

Doc Junker drove faster than usual, skidding slightly on corners as he took the icy country roads on faith. What time was the booze delivery scheduled for? It was already almost midnight. He'd cracked the window open a tad so the cold air would keep him awake, but adrenaline was doing a fine job all by itself.

Despite what he'd told Martha, Junker wasn't counting on Graziano Fellini beating him to the rendezvous. He planned to park the Tin Lizzie, reconnoiter as best he could without confronting any of the bootleggers, and wait for the cavalry to arrive.

Naturally, that plan didn't include a flat tire. It happened just as he was on the bumpy approach road to the Tate Farm, a few yards shy of the main gate. The vehicle veered left until he yanked it back under control and killed the engine. While Junker sat still catching his breath after his near encounter with the deep ditch on the side of the dirt road, a truck pulled up next to him.

"Now what's a fine middle-aged doctor like you doing in a place like this?"

The falsely jovial tones of Big Bruce Donaldson sent prickles of unease down Junker's neck. He decided to tell part of the truth. "I heard there were swell gatherings out this way on certain evenings. I came out to join the party."

"Well, well. We'll just escort you on in, won't we boys? Hop out and step into the truck, Illinois. And don't try anything funny."

Junker climbed out of his car, allowed two of Donaldson's men to frisk him and take away the pistol he'd brought. Then they shoved him into the back of the four-seater cabin.

The tall man in the front seat turned around and grinned at Junker. "Our favorite Doctor, eh? Should make things more interesting," said "Han the Hun" Stoltman.

Junker figured he didn't have to answer that.

The truck pulled into the center of the yard, between the two main barns and a couple of smaller storage sheds.

Everyone piled out. Junker discovered that the skinny guy had a gun pointed at his stomach.

"What shall I do with the doc, boss?"

"Nothing...yet," said Big Bruce. "When is our delivery due?"

"Any minute now." That was another man, a chunky thirty-something specimen in a wool suit and battered fedora. Wispy curls of pepper-and-salt hair stuck out from under the hat, almost hiding the eyes that were small and mean. He was one of about ten tough-looking men waiting nearby.

Two more men opened the double doors to the biggest barn. From where Junker was standing, he could see it was packed to the roofs with crates with the Blue Fire prairie grass logo stamped on the front.

Big Bruce came over to Junker and put an arm around his shoulders. "How about the grand tour, Doc? I figure that's why you really came out here. Lemme show you how we store the hooch and home remedies that go out to speaks all over Champaign County..."

That was when Junker realized that if Fellini and his men didn't get here on time, he was a dead man. No way was this crook going to show him the whole operation—and let him see the faces of his henchman—and leave Junker alive to tell the tale. He'd already recognized Dick Tate, Bill Jonich, Harry Whitely, and several of his former patients.

But he couldn't help totting things up in his mind as Big Bruce showed off his stock. Something like forty cases of Canadian bonded whiskey on the left side of the barn; just as many cases of gin and beer on the other. Jamaican rum in the middle. The back of the barn was reserved for the tonics and medicines. Junker spotted a whole row of that damn cough syrup that had killed young Marcus. His blood began to heat up as his body debated whether to fight or flee.

A rumble of engines alerted the gang to the arrival of the expected delivery. Four trucks pulled into the yard. Everyone gathered around, and with hardly any direction from Big Bruce, organized themselves in four lines to unload each truck and pass the new crates from man to man and stack them in the big barn.

Where in tarnation was Fellini? This was the moment to arrive and catch the bootleggers red-handed! Junker had never felt so helpless. Here he was, in the middle of an operation that supplied the entire county with illegal hooch and dangerous home remedies and he couldn't do a damn thing! While his eyes swiveled around looking for either a weapon or a way out of the yard, his mind went back to its adding machine. Thirty new cases of whiskey, five of gin...

A battered Pathfinder pulled into the yard. Out jumped a tall man Junker recognized as the original of the photo in Stipes' pocket: Bernie Shelton from "Bloody Williamson" County in Little Egypt, down south. Then a small, skinny man wearing a Thomas splint got out from the driver's side and sauntered over to give directions to the men unloading the last truck.

Big Bruce left Junker's side abruptly, leaving him with the gangster toting the gun trained on his gut. A heated discussion ensued. Junker watched cynically as all the men, including Bruce, deferred to the small man in the splint. The small man eventually noticed Junker and limped toward him.

"Whaaal! Lookee what we have here. My good friend Illinois Junker!"

"Well, look what the cat dragged in! Nathan Donaldson! What are you doing out here at Tate Farm? You oughtta be at home resting that leg of yours!" Junker said.

"Says you. Fortunately, I got associates who can drive me around."

"Nathan, if I'd figured out you were the one really in charge of this operation sooner, you'd be behind bars already."

"Me?" Donaldson laughed. "Why, you don't have any proof at all that I'm involved. Brother Bruce here is the fella who takes all the heat."

"I figure he's just window dressing. You're the real McCoy, and I do have proof. I have your initials on liquor receipts." Damned if he'd say how he'd come by them.

"That so?" said Nathan. "And I guess you think you can prove from a couple of lousy initials that it's my handwriting? Ha. I don't suppose you brought them with you?"

"Think I'm stupid? They're at home in a safe place. You know, Nathan, the illegal hooch is one thing—there are lots of other bootleggers like you around the state—but the home remedies, that's gotta stop."

"Why? They bring in good income." Nathan crossed his arms and bounced a little on his good leg.

Junker shoved his nose into Donaldson's face. "Because, you darned ignorant grave-looter, those concoctions are killing people! I've lost one patient, a young boy, and damn near lost my own son to cocaine addiction!"

Nathan stopped grinning and bouncing. "Don't you call me a grave-looter. And I'm sure I don't know what's in them bottles. I just sell the stuff."

"Yeah? Well, in the eyes of the law, you should know what's in them! Coke, morphine, way too much grain alcohol, and a whole lot of other stuff that's not been tested, especially in combination! It's the drug interactions that are making people sick or outright killing them—and you are responsible!" Junker roared.

Something in one of the barns behind him fell over with a clang.

"Boss, someone's in there!" Dick Tate yelled.

Nathan spoke without turning around, "Well you and Billy go get 'em!"

Billy and Dick didn't get very far. Junker heard Frank yelp and then a crash as glass broke on one of the parked cars. He spun around in time to see his daughter, Anna, throw a whiskey bottle at the two young men.

"Hey! That's expensive stock! Someone grab that little

bitch!" cried Nathan.

Junker heard more breaking glass as Anna gave a good account of herself.

Nathan signaled to Bernie's men and several rushed the barn.

Two scruffy fellas reappeared dragging Anna Junker and deposited her next to her father.

Big Bruce greeted her appearance with enthusiasm. "The little blondie! I was hoping for a chance to get to know you better! Now, what would you be doing out here?"

Nathan said, "I bet she's not alone. Search that barn!" Billy and Dick ran back into the barn while several other men spread out around the perimeter.

Anna, looking disheveled but defiant, nodded at her parent. A small amount of blood trickled from her right hand.

"You're bleeding!"

"It's just a cut—I tried to fend off one of the men with a broken whiskey bottle."

"I wish to hell you'd stay home like you were supposed to," Junker grumbled. "Now we're both in trouble."

"I think Ben got away," she whispered. "He'll get help."

The sputtering sound of a car starting confirmed that someone had reached the parked cars. Dick and several other men raced along the farm road to intercept Ben.

Junker ground his teeth. Now he had two more people to worry about in addition to himself.

Dick Tate returned empty-handed. "I caught a glimpse of him. It was Ben Keck—the same sap who was out here stealing invoices."

"Friend of yours, right? You sure know how to pick 'em," said Nathan. "Bernie, which one of your associates messed up that robbery at the Keck house?"

Bernie shoved his fedora back on his head and smiled slowly. "It was Carlson. He ain't here tonight. Took off after he got away from the feds." He sauntered over to Anna and her father. He looked Anna up and down and then reached over and squeezed a breast with one hand. Anna spat at him.

The gangster laughed. "A real spitfire! Say, how 'bout you

give me this little lady instead of the hooch you owe me, Nathan? I could have a good time with this one."

Junker put Anna on the other side of him. "Leave her alone. She has nothing to do with your business—she followed me out here."

Nathan drawled, "That so? Well, we can do whatever we want with the two of you. Why don't we start with…"

Shots rang out and Nathan never did finish his sentence. Instantly all the bootleggers were in motion, firing back at unseen shooters in the bushes and taking cover.

As soon as Junker felt the gun removed from his back, he grabbed Anna and pulled her behind the barn where she and Ben had hidden. He pushed Anna down flat and covered her body with his own, shifting his head so he could peer around the corner of the barn at foot level.

"Ow! Papa, you're squashing me!"

"Shhh! I don't want you to get shot."

Anna lay still. "Okay, then you have to tell me every single thing you see."

"It's crazy out there. Nathan is getting away—so is Bernie Shelton. Looks like Fellini and his cops just arrived. Whoops, there's Ben!"

Once again, Anna struggled to rise. Her father put a hand on her neck and pressed her flat.

"Papa! Let me up!"

"Ben is fine," said her father without moving. "He's staying with the vehicles, probably because Fellini told him to. Oh, no…Dick Tate is down. He's not moving."

This was too much for Anna. She gave her father an almighty shove so he rolled over. She scrambled to her hands and knees and moved slightly away from the barn's outer wall so he couldn't pounce on her again and she could see for herself.

The shooting continued, a regular firestorm as the gangsters emptied their weapons and the police fought back. "Papa, I think Dick's dead!" Anna said in an agonized whisper.

After watching blood trickle down Dick's motionless face, Junker had reached the same conclusion. "Wait until Fellini takes control," he said, once again restraining his daughter from bolting into the open. "Then we can both go help."

From his post behind the police vehicles, Ben saw Dick fall. His heart jumped in his chest, but the shooting was so fierce he didn't dare move. He had never really liked Dick Tate—he was a slippery, unreliable fella—but he was a contemporary and a friend of Frank's. They'd all been in Big Grove High School together.

Ben seethed. The fact that Fellini hadn't let him carry a weapon made him feel even more useless.

He waited in an agony of impatience while Fellini and his men rounded up the gangsters who hadn't managed to slip away. Big Bruce Donaldson was under arrest, thank goodness, as was "Han the Hun" Stoltman. He couldn't see Nathan—he was such a weasel, he'd probably gotten clean away.

Finally, Fellini motioned Ben over.

Ben approached Dick's motionless body. Anna was already there, crouched next to Dick's bloody head. She looked up at Ben, her eyes full of tears.

"Ben...I know he wasn't your buddy, like Frank, but no one should die this y...young," she said softly, choking on the last word.

Ben knelt down beside her and took Dick's limp hand in his own. He felt almost as guilty about Dick's death as he did about Frank's, but for different reasons. He couldn't mourn Dick—he was almost glad he was dead. Dick Tate'd been the ringleader, the wise guy, the one who'd roped Frank into doping and boozing to excess. But Ben knew Frank was a follower, and he'd followed Dick because Ben, his best friend from elementary school, had given him the cold shoulder after a run-in over a girl. And then he got so busy with his photography and seeing Anna...So that meant Ben was responsible to some degree; if only he'd spent more time with Frank and Dick instead of writing them off as losers and boozers, maybe he could have headed off these senseless killings...he felt like such a shit.

He wasn't aware that tears were dripping off his nose until a hand fell on his shoulder. "It is not your fault, Ben. Whatever you think."

Ben looked up into Doc Junker's kind face. "Sir, it is partly my fault. I ignored Dick because I didn't like him very much, and I got too busy to spend much time with Frank..."

Anna, stepping up to Ben's other side and pulling him up to a standing position, backed her father up. "You are not your friend's keeper. You cared, but you couldn't control where he went or who his friends were."

Junker helped Ben get up. "Dick made his own choices—and so did Frank. Now come along, Ben. I'm driving you both home."

Chapter Twenty-five
Friday, late morning

At eleven the next morning, Junker made sure Anna was still safely in bed before he left to meet Fellini at the Steamroom. He wasn't convinced they'd succeeded in rounding up all the local gangsters and he didn't want his nosy daughter and her boyfriend to have any more opportunities to get into trouble.

"Any news?" he asked as Fellini led him around back of the smithy.

"Yep. The feds have hauled away all the hooch from Tate Farm and rounded up the rest of Nathan and Bruce's men. Nathan Donaldson wrecked his car trying to get away and ended up in hospital with a broken collarbone, four smashed ribs, and a lung puncture."

"Serves him right," said Junker sourly. "To think I sort of trusted that guy. Well, not about artifacts or taking care of archaeological sites. But I thought he was basically okay. What about Bernie Shelton?"

"Got clean away. You realize this is one of Charlie Birger's buddies? The worst of the worst. Makes Capone's gang look like Sunday school kids. Bernie must have had a vehicle parked farther way that he got to before we could. Those Little Egypt hooligans just vanished like smoke. All we got were the locals."

Fellini unlocked the back door of the smithy. "What we're looking for is probably hidden storage for cartons of illegal hooch," he said. "The bootleggers have to have a downtown storeroom for distribution to the speaks."

Junker started poking around. The dark and gloomy smithy

displayed organized chaos—blacksmithing tongs and hammers placed in racks near the anvil, coal bins positioned near the fire for easy loading, iron bar stock neatly stacked for fashioning into fireplace tools, knives, and candlesticks. A thin layer of coal dust covered everything, and Junker could hardly see until he unlatched a couple of shutters and threw them open to let in watery sunlight.

"Huh," he said, looking around. "I suppose all this is connected to the steam laundry and the speakeasy next door since Donaldson owns the entire complex, right?"

Graziano Fellini nodded. "Big Bruce told me that much. But I'm not sure he gave me all his keys. He looked a bit shifty when he handed over this lot." He jingled the key ring in his pocket. "I bet there's a least one more key hidden on a hook somewhere that very few people know about."

Junker nodded. His grandfather, who'd gotten a little paranoid in his later years, had stored keys in peculiar places, such as behind farm equipment in little wall niches that required awkward reaching to get at. He strolled over to the corner nearest the anvil, where racks of hammers lined the wall. Hmm. Was that a depression in the wall, up behind the biggest hammer? He reached up. It was, but there was no key—and no hook. Fellini caught on right away and checked behind other vertical tool racks.

They had no luck until Junker remembered another trick of his grandfather's. "If you want to hide something, put it above or below eye level. It takes most folks longer to check places that aren't right in front of their eyeballs." He'd demonstrated by showing Junker how the combination to his safe was taped to the back of a desk leg at floor level.

What about the back of the anvil? Sure enough, near the floor was a little box taped to the base of the anvil, almost covered with coal dust. Inside was a key.

"Aha!" said Junker, holding them up. "Now to find the door this goes to."

Fellini said, "If it were me, I'd keep the key in a different room from the hidden storeroom."

"Good point," Junker replied. "Let's go through to the

steam laundry and see what we can find."

Their reasoning proved correct. Fifteen minutes later the two men uncovered a door behind a rack of coats that awaited returning customers. It led to a narrow, windowless room between the laundry and the smithy that no one could detect from the outside. One end was stacked with Blue Fire crates, but the other end held a surprise: a small-scale still with a chimney pipe that exited the ceiling near the vents for the steam laundry and the larger chimney for the coal fire. Near the still, whiskey bottles and Blue Fire labels were neatly stacked. Huh. Just enough for a small personal supply of hooch!

Junker shook his head with admiration. "Clever, really clever."

Fellini asked, "How so, Illinois?"

Junker explained. "The smell of hot mash and smoke from the still are disguised by the steam from the laundry and the stink and smoke of the coal fire next door. You'd have to have a really good nose to pick out the corn mash from all the other stuff. Looks like Bruce—and maybe his nephew, Frank, were producing their own supply and cutting out the middleman."

Fellini smiled. "I never doubted Big Bruce's deviousness. But what really surprised me was brother Nathan's leadership. I never had him pegged as the head honcho."

"Neither did I. He acts so whiney and gutless sometimes—it is really hard to see him as a career criminal or a gang leader. Frank's shooting was an accident, right?"

"That's what his uncle told us," said Fellini. Poor sap got between Bernie Shelton and someone from down south he was trying to take out."

"Poor Frank. Say, we still don't know which gangster killed Stipes. I assume the motive was because Harry was asking too many questions about Blue Fire Distributors?"

"Almost certainly."

Junker said, "I'm willing to bet Nathan ordered one of his men to poison Stipes' medicine when Stipes wasn't looking. Since Frank Donaldson wasn't the sort of fella who could do anything subtle, it must have been one of Nathan or Big Bruce's other employees."

"Well, I haven't succeeded in questioning Nathan as much as I want to—the nurses and doctors want him to rest. But I plan to turn him inside out as soon as they let me at him," said Fellini with a glint in his eye.

Junker smiled. "Here's hoping they make you police chief. You've got what it takes, Graziano." He shook Fellini's hand and departed for Tate Farm. Now that the excise agents were through, he planned to spend a little time evaluating the burial site. Junker felt it in his gut—this site was a major find. With Nathan behind bars, he and Tommy could take their time—and do the archaeology carefully and methodically for a change.

By the time he arrived at Tate Farm, the sun had warmed the ground and dispelled the icy mist. Junker didn't kid himself that he could do a full-scale excavation only a few days before Christmas, but he could assess what was there and how to go about it when the weather improved. And the earth thawed.

He slid on his galoshes over his good shoes and tramped over to the stream.

Someone had been there before him—the area was disturbed. But Junker could see a femur and some ribs peeking out of the dirt. He looked closer, gently scraping away clods of dirt from the skeleton and saw a bit of shell. Trade beads? Hmm. So it was a burial all right, but what was the context? Were there other bodies here? Was it a mound with multiple or a single burial, perhaps near a settlement? Junker could hardly wait for spring to come so he could clear a larger area.

He sat back on his heels. What could he do, with just a trowel, while the deeper dirt was frozen? Well, the fella before him—probably Nathan—had made a mess. Junker could clean that up a bit. He set to work straightening the sides of the pit that the Donaldsons had started, scraping thawing clods of earth away until he had a straight profile. The sun obliged by going behind a cloud so he could actually see colors in the dirt: a clear layer of darker dirt or ash that separately the layer with the bones from the one above the burial. And his efforts were rewarded with two more artifacts: a potsherd protruding from the wall, in the top layer, and part of a carved pipe.

Junker did a quick sketch of his profile and the location of the potsherd and the pipe in relationship to the skeleton. Then he pulled out the potsherd and noticed right away that it was a rim, decorated with semi-circular marks and slashes that could have been made by a sharp stick. They formed a pleasing pattern, and reminded Junker of a large vessel he's seen in Fulton County.

The pipe was a real find. A carved bird—maybe a hawk—in red pipestone, polished and well preserved, sitting on a slightly curved platform that was broken on one end.

He slipped the two artifacts into his field bag and put away the trowel. Whipping out his camera, he took several pictures to record what he had seen and done. He'd ask young Ben to develop them for him.

As he thought about unwelcome visitors, Junker kicked some of the loose dirt back into his pit and piled some branches over the area. No telling who would happen along and mess with the dig before spring. His cover-up wouldn't stop someone who'd already seen the site, but with a good layer of snow over it, it might deter arrowhead hunters until spring.

Junker was excited. The two layers he'd identified plus the burial indicated a promising site with at least two time periods represented. He'd do some more reading about the artifacts over the winter and maybe recruit someone he could trust to help him dig as soon as the ground softened up.

Junker still didn't know if the site was a proper mound, but he thought it should be named after Frank Donaldson. Frank's Mound had a nice ring to it. And digging it up would be a labor of love and a tribute to the young man who had died before his time.

Maybe Ben Keck would help him.

Chapter Twenty-Six
The Sunday before Christmas

Anna perched on the end of Ben's bed at the Keck house. Her task, given to her by Linda Keck, was to cheer up Ben and convince him to get dressed and come downstairs for a celebratory Sunday dinner with the Junker and Keck families. From the bedroom, strategically positioned over the kitchen with a view of the back alley, Anna could smell roast chicken with sage stuffing and her mother's apple pies cooling on the counter. A hubbub of voices told her they were missing the fun.

"Ben, I know you're depressed about Frank. I would be if it were one of my best friends who'd been killed. It's okay to be sad."

Ben sighed and shifted under the covers. "I just wish I didn't feel so guilty. Like I should have done something different. And Dick Tate shouldn't have died either."

"You want to take care of your friends—that's wonderful. But you're not God, you can't prevent bad things from happening."

"I'm not sure God—if God exists—can, either."

They'd already had several discussions about religion. Neither Ben nor Anna was sure which of their parents' beliefs they shared and which they were ready to throw out. Anna said she believed in God, but was quite sure *He* looked nothing like her grandfather. Ben favored a Great Spirit of some kind— something that was everywhere, in every rock and tree and river, and couldn't be described by ordinary mortals. Together, they agreed they were neither Lutheran nor Methodist, but something wholly new.

"Ben, Papa wanted me to tell you he's been out to the archaeological site on Tate Farm again. He thinks it's a burial mound, a major find that should be excavated properly and published. He wants to call it Frank's Mound."

Ben looked up. "Really? That's very good of him. But nothing can bring Frank back. I know he was a weak person who made mistakes, but he was my friend. What bothers me is that his life was just cut off, like he was a squashed bug or something. It just seems so rotten that Frank gets no second chance. He wanted to be a painter, did you know that?"

Anna's mouth dropped open. "No, I had no idea! Oils? Watercolor?"

"Everything. He had a little studio in his father's attic. Frank was good, really good. He did exquisite landscapes—all sky, with grasses and barns down at the bottom. And detailed studies of birds. He could have been a major artist—if his miserable dad and crooked uncle hadn't had other plans for him."

Anna took his hand and he hung on tightly. They sat quietly, listening to the tinkle of glasses and crockery downstairs as the table was set. Her mind drifted between the two problems of how to make Ben feel better and what to get him for Christmas...

Anna said slowly, "Maybe...maybe you can sort of make up for Frank's death."

"Huh? How can I make up for someone dying?"

"I'm not sure exactly. I mean, if you follow your dream to become a photographer, that's living the kind of artistic life he would have wanted, isn't it?"

Ben stared at her. "Sort of like a trade? His life for mine?"

"Yeah, maybe. You don't want to work in your father's furniture store—you told me so. If you refuse to follow that path and go your own way, why Frank will cheer you on from wherever he is now."

"I don't know whether I believe your crazy reasoning, but I like it." Suddenly he smiled. "There's something I haven't told you, Anna."

"What?"

"You remember that photo I sent into the Big Grove Gazette photo contest? The one of smoke rising over the Steamroom at dawn? Well, it won First Prize."

"Ben, how super!" Anna bounced on the bed.

"I think I'll take that as a positive sign." Ben shoved the covers back. "I'm getting up. You scoot downstairs and tell them I'll be five minutes."

The party in the festively decorated Keck dining room included the two families, Grandpa Junker, Tommy Crouch, and Graziano Fellini. A feast covered the long table that was lit with tall red candles around a pine-and-holly centerpiece. After Linda Keck said grace, everyone attacked the roast chicken, mashed potatoes and gravy, green beans with *spaetzle*, and homemade sourdough bread with gusto. When Linda passed her homemade, herb-infused vodka around the table, Martha startled her friends and relatives by taking a small glass.

"Mama!" said Anna. "I can't believe you're sipping vodka— and doing it like it's something commonplace for you!"

"Yeah," said her brother Hans, round-eyed. "Aren't you always telling us hooch is bad for us?"

Martha traded an amused glance with her husband. "Well, maybe working in a roadhouse for a few days adjusted my attitude."

"Bout time," Grandpa said. "A little high-quality booze never hurt anyone. Taken in moderation, of course." He winked at Anna.

Linda Keck roared with laughter. "Good for you, Martha! But why did you do it? And how did you manage with all these young children underfoot?"

Illinois Junker said with quiet pride, "Martha decided to help the WCTU collect evidence for illegal distribution of booze by becoming a barmaid. I didn't know anything about it until Tommy and I saw her at Kelly's Roadhouse. She made me keep my mouth shut and served us whiskey like she was born to it." He grinned. "And she made a right pretty barmaid, too."

Martha turned as pink as her twinset.

"I knew about it," said Anna.

Ben looked at her with raised eyebrows. "You didn't tell me!"

"She had to tell me since I was babysitting. But she made me swear not to tell anyone else."

Graziano said, "Martha helped us solve the case. She stole some receipts that gave us the link between Blue Fire Distributors and Nathan Donaldson."

"Mama stole somethin'?" asked Franz. "Wow! Are you going to jail, Mama?"

Everyone laughed. "You don't go to jail if you're helping the police, son," said Junker. But don't let it give you any ideas— Martha is not going back to the roadhouse. Not as an employee, at least." He looked at his wife with a raised eyebrow.

"I might go with Earl one night and have a cocktail," she replied with a twinkle in her eye. "And Jo and Gerry Cunningham just might come out with us."

Matthew Keck shook his head and took another helping of potatoes. "Never thought I'd see the day," he said with a chuckle.

Grandpa Junker thumped the table with his glass. "That's fine, but I want to know more about the bootlegging gang. What about Nathan Donaldson? And did you find the rest of the hooch?"

Fellini obliged. "Nathan confesto arranging Stipes' murder. A pal of his who frequented the same speak waited until Stipes was distracted by an argument, pinched his flask long enough to doctor it, and slipped it back into Stipes' pocket. Since the extra digitalis was added to the prescription medicine he took a quarter of an hour later, the overdose killed him. Nathan will be put away for a good long time for that, as well as pushing lousy booze and dangerous home remedies on the entire county over the last two years."

"So my buddy Frank had nothing to do with the murder?" asked Ben.

"That is correct."

Ben sighed and exchanged a smile with Anna, who was seated across the table from him.

Grandpa smacked the table again, this time with his hand. "So what about the hooch?"

"The secret storage room, the liquor distribution center for downtown Big Grove, was next to the Steamroom," said Junker. "Fellini and I found it Friday after we rummaged around the smithy and found the key, then we poked around the steam laundry until we discovered the hidden door." He explained about the still for the Donaldson's private supply.

"That explains why Frank was so secretive about the stuff he carried in his hip flask!" said Ben. "I knew there was something fishy about that! He must have helped his uncle make the whiskey."

"No doubt," said Fellini. "I think young Frank did pretty much whatever his uncle Bruce said. Nathan had his own fish to fry—doesn't seem like he paid a whole lot of attention to his son."

"I know—Frank always said his Dad had no time for him. He needed someone to tell him what to do. At least he will get an archaeological site named after him," said Ben with a grateful look at Doc Junker. "Officer Fellini, I understand Blue Fire was the distributor for all the booze, but where was it produced? They didn't have a factory around here, did they?" asked Ben.

"No, they didn't," answered Junker. "The production was in Little Egypt, run by the Shelton gang. That was the connection suggested by the photo of Bernie Shelton found in Stipes' pocket. The Shelton family controls liquor manufacturing all over the southern part of the state, and they were trying to expand to the north. They also run gambling joints and prostitution rings in five cities. They make Capone's Chicago activities look almost tame by comparison."

"Nathan and Bruce got in over their heads dealing with the Sheltons," said Fellini. "They were trying to siphon off some of the business here in Champaign County so they could make a bigger profit—without giving the Sheltons their fair share. They're lucky they weren't bumped off."

"Whaal," said Grandpa, tipping his chair back so it rested precariously on two legs. "That just leaves me with one question."

"What's that, Father?" asked Junker.

"Why didn't you trade Anna for some decent booze while you had the chance?"

"Thomas Earl Junker!" cried Martha

"Grandpa! I wouldn't have gone with those men!" Anna said indignantly.

"Of course you wouldn't, darlin.' But it would make such a good story to tell my friends," replied Grandpa. "Linda, how about you pass the vodka?"

Sarah Underhill Wisseman writes two series of archaeological mysteries. The first contemporary series stars Lisa Donahue, an archaeologist and museum curator. The Bootlegger's Nephew begins the second series of historical (Prohibition) mysteries featuring physician and amateur archaeologist Illinois Junker and his nineteen-year-old flapper daughter Anna.

Sarah hadn't a clue that she wanted to be an archaeologist until she traveled to Israel right after her freshman year in college. There she ate felafel, fell in love with Jerusalem, camped illegally on Masada, and spent a month at the excavation of biblical Beersheba. Once hooked by archaeology, she returned for her junior year at Tel Aviv University, an experience that changed her life.

Back in the U.S., she completed her B.A. in Anthropology at Harvard University and volunteered in the Harvard Semitic Museum and the Peabody Museum in Cambridge, Massachusetts. Then she left her home state of Massachusetts and moved to Philadelphia for graduate school in Classical and Near Eastern Archaeology at Bryn Mawr College. There she met a medical student, Charlie Wisseman, who became her husband in 1975.

Sarah had just finished her M.A. and was working on her Ph.D when Charlie landed his first job as a pathologist working for the Public Health Service in Cincinnati. She seized the opportunity to learn more about art conservation by volunteering in the laboratory at the Cincinnati Art Museum.

When her husband migrated to a job in Urbana, Illinois, Sarah became a curator, grant writer, and fundraiser at the World Heritage Museum, located in a creepy, fourth-floor attic at the University of Illinois. Somehow she survived the experience of working there while raising two children, Nick and Emily. Then Sarah was lured away from the museum world into archaeological science. She currently directs the Program on Ancient Technologies and Archaeological Materials (ATAM), also at the University of Illinois.

The Bootlegger's Nephew is Sarah's fifth mystery. The earlier Lisa Donahue mysteries include: Bound for Eternity (Finalist in the 2004 St. Martin's Press Malice Domestic contest for Best First Traditional Mystery, published in 2005); The Dead Sea Codex (2006); The Fall of Augustus (2009), and The House of the Sphinx (2009).

Sarah currently lives in Champaign, Illinois, with her husband and two cats. For more information about her novels, short stories, and articles, visit www.sarahwisseman.com

Made in the USA
Lexington, KY
13 March 2012